A PELICAN BEACH AFFAIR

PELICAN BEACH SERIES BOOK THREE

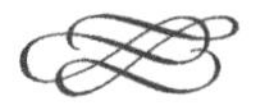

MICHELE GILCREST

GET A FREE EBOOK!

Would you like a FREE ebook? JOIN Michele's newsletter to receive information about new releases, giveaways, and special promotions! To say thank you, I'll send you a FREE copy of The Inn at Pelican Beach. Sign up today!

https://dl.bookfunnel.com/wr9wvokoin

PAYTON

It was late February, and I was no closer to securing a venue for the wedding than when Cole proposed. It's not that I didn't try. Cole even suggested that we get married at a country club. But putting on a fanfare that was more for the people and less intimate for us seemed out of character. With the wedding plans still up in the air, the family shifted their attention to my sister, Rebecca. She was two days overdue and ready to give birth at any moment. The only thing that remained steady and predictable at the moment was my livelihood at the store.

"Payton, I know that I'm just an assistant, but I have some ideas for the store that might really help boost your online presence." Natalie helped pack up the equipment we had on the beach and continued to share.

"What did you have in mind?"

"You're already taking things to the next level with your style of photography. Just take today's photoshoot, for example. You literally set up an antique couch on the beach in February to take engagement photos. Do you know how romantic it looked with the ocean as the backdrop behind them? You gave the couple some of the most fashion-forward ideas for their outfits and the props. It was a total success!"

"Why, thank you, Natalie. But what does that have to do with my online presence?"

"Well, imagine the buzz you could create about Picture Perfect on social media? The same way models show off designer clothing on the runway, you can show off your creative photography business on the internet. What if people could follow your posts and see snapshots of your creative locations? What if you could go live or post instant stories to give people the behind the scenes look at your work as a photographer?"

"I can tell you've been putting a lot of thought into this."

"I'm sorry. The deeper I dive into my marketing classes, the more I can't help myself."

"Don't be sorry. You have a lot of great ideas. It's definitely worth looking into. Right now, I just have a website, but social media may be the way to go."

I zipped up my last piece of equipment and dusted the sand off my bags. The temperature was in the lower 70's, which felt relatively cool by the water.

"How about we get these bags in the van, and you help me with the couch. Once we get back, we can talk about your ideas a little further."

"Sounds good to me."

I loved Natalie's enthusiasm. We worked so well together. I feared that she would graduate and leave Pelican Beach and the store behind soon. On the drive back, we listened to country music and enjoyed each other's company.

On the other side of the road, a parade of emergency vehicles whizzed by.

"I wonder what happened. Whenever I see that many cop

cars and fire trucks speeding by, I always say a quick prayer," Natalie said.

"That's not a bad idea. I'm not sure where they're headed, but hopefully, people will get out of their way with all the sirens blaring."

We watched more vehicles pass us by. Before long, we were back at the store and began unloading the van.

"If you grab this end of the couch, I'll go ahead and grab the other," I said.

"Got it."

We carefully carried the couch to the back and put everything in its place. Natalie switched my front sign to open while I took care of a few odds and ends around the store.

For the first time ever, my coo-coo clock from the thrift store began to chime.

"Coo-coo, coo-coo."

Natalie and I laughed after being startled by it. I'd always admired the clock, but everyone knew it's functionality was limited, until now.

"It looks like you gave up on your clock a little too soon." Natalie dusted around the clock's trim.

"How about that. I guess I did. Now, if we could only figure out how to limit the coo-coo chime to sound on the hour, we'd be in good shape. I'll have Cole take a look at it. Maybe he can figure it out."

Natalie brought over her laptop.

"Do you have a moment to take a look at what I was talking about earlier?"

"Sure. Let's pull up a couple of stools."

"Okay, here's what I was thinking." Her enthusiasm was through the roof.

"If you look at the setup of this page, you can upload a picture from this morning at the click of a button. Include one of the shots with the couch and all of the staging. Then you can write a quick blurb underneath. Something like 'props from today's engagement photos,' or 'looking for a creative photographer for your next event?' You know what to say... basically anything else that inspires you and describes your business."

"Natalie, you might be on to something. That's not a bad idea."

"It's a way to stay connected with your customers."

"I like it, and I can't think of a better person to spearhead this new project than you! Maybe you can help to at least get it up and running for me?"

"I was hoping you would say that. This is my specialty. My boyfriend recently shared some new features with me that I think you'll love."

"Natalie, I didn't know you had a boyfriend. What's his name?"

"Brandon."

Her cheeks started to blush.

"Do tell. How long have you been together? And where did you meet?"

"We've been dating for almost a year. I have a study group that meets weekly at the library, and he works there. Over time I noticed him always fumbling and going out of his way to help me find books, so I took that as a sign that he might be interested. He's a bit of a nerd, but I'd prefer his type over the arrogant jock types any day of the week."

"I hear ya on that one. Nobody wants to waste time with a jerk."

She smiled.

"So have you started making plans for what you want to do in the spring when you graduate?"

"I'd love to move to New York," Natalie said.

This was precisely what I was afraid of. It was the very

thing my sister Abby had warned me about when I hired a college student. I still believe that any part-time help could leave just as easily. But, if Natalie left, I knew I would miss her.

She continued. "They have so many fortune five hundred companies that could really help pave the way for my marketing career. However, it's a dream that will have to be deferred for now. My mom has been ill, and I really need to stay close and to help take care of her."

"Natalie, I'm so sorry. I didn't know. You didn't say a word."

"It's okay, Payton. I try to put all my personal life matters to the side when I'm here and at school to stay focused. It's not your fault."

"I appreciate it, but still. I'm sure you just see me as your boss, but please know that I'm here and care about you should there be anything you want to talk about."

"Thanks, Payton. I love working with you. I really do."

"I love you working here. The thought of you ever leaving makes me sad, but please know that I would be understanding when the time comes."

The bells on the front door signaled as a customer entered in.

"Welcome to Picture Perfect. How can I help you?" Natalie greeted a woman who approached the counter and laid her bag down. She was gorgeous with long dark hair, fitted jeans, and tall boots.

"Hi there. I'm here to make an appointment to take a few pictures for my modeling portfolio."

"Hi, I'm Payton Matthews, owner of Picture Perfect. I'm going to let Natalie pull out some sample packages that we have to offer. I'll let you look through and choose the best options, and then we can get you set up with an appointment."

"Sounds great."

Natalie opened up a few drawers to pull the pamphlets that we needed.

"Man, it was crazy getting over here. The traffic is backed up for miles trying to get into Pelican Beach." She seemed flustered, so I offered her a bottle of water.

"I wonder what's going on," I said.

"You didn't hear? It's all over the radio. There was a major fire over on the northern end of the beach. One of the mansions over there was undergoing some remodeling, and somehow a fire broke out. Firefighters are trying to get the fire under control, but a few of the crew members are trapped on the upstairs level."

I instantly felt uneasy. As she was talking, I was scrambling to remember the name of the street where my fiancé was working on his renovation. I knew it was on the beach's northern end, but I couldn't remember the details.

"Ma'am, are you alright? You don't look like you feel so good," she said.

"I'm sorry. What station did you say you heard this on?"

"I'm sure you can catch it if you turn to 1010 on the AM stations."

Natalie took over while I went to the back. I turned on the radio and dialed the numbers to the right station just in time to conclude the weather.

'That wraps up our weather. Now let's hear a few updates on our local news. Firefighters are still working hard to contain the mansion fire over in Forest Hill Estates. It's been reported that they're trying to rescue those trapped on the top floor. More details to come as the situation unfolds.'

I tried Cole's cell phone several times but continued to get his voicemail. Even though I had this feeling of unrest, I tried to remain calm. I decided to dial his mother to see if she heard anything.

"Hi, Alice. This is Payton. How are you?"

"Payton, I was just about to call you. Have you seen the news?"

"I haven't seen it, but one of my customers told me about the fire. Have you heard from Cole by any chance?"

"No, I haven't. I tried his phone several times, and he hasn't answered. I thought I would try you to see if you knew anything," she said.

"Well, we were both thinking along the same lines. That's precisely why I called you. Alice, I know Cole mentioned that he had a job out on the northern side of the beach. But did he share any other specifics with you?"

"He did mention that he was working on a mansion project. That's what's making me nervous about the news report. I'm sure there are many mansions in Forest Hill. But, how many of them are getting their house renovated?"

Nail-biting while staring around the room didn't bring me any closer to a solution.

"Payton?"

"Yes, I'm here, Alice. I'm wondering if I should drive over to Forest Hill. This way, I can confirm if Cole's there by looking for his truck."

"That's a good idea. Emmie and I can ride with you if you'd like."

Even though Cole's daughter, Emmie, was extremely mature for her age, the last thing I would want is to upset her.

"It's okay, Alice. I think we better exercise caution with Emmie."

"You're right. We don't want to make her worry. Especially if we find out there was nothing to worry about in the first place."

"Exactly. I just wish Cole would answer his phone. I don't

want to belabor this any longer. I'm grabbing my keys and leaving now. I'll call you as soon as I know more."

"Likewise. I love you, Payton."

"I love you, too, Alice."

I grabbed my keys and returned to the front to explain the situation to Natalie. She was wrapping things up with the customer who came in to book an appointment.

"Ladies, my apologies. I had to take an important phone call. Is there anything I can help you with, or are you all set?"

"I think we're good. I decided to go with a large portfolio. I'll be back on Saturday to take the pictures."

"Wonderful. I'm sorry, I think I missed your name earlier."

"It's Amanda."

"Amanda, thank you. I'm looking forward to our appointment."

"So am I. I'll see you then."

"Sounds good."

As soon as she left, I proceeded to give Natalie the run down.

"Oh, no. I hope it's just a coincidence—no wonder you started to look so nervous. Please let me know what I can do to help," Natalie said.

"If you're able to hold down the fort here at the store, that would be the most helpful."

"Yes, of course."

"If, for some reason, I'm not back within the next two hours, I'll gladly pay you any overtime."

"Payton, don't worry about it. Just go. I want you to be able to put your mind at ease."

"Thank you, Natalie."

No sooner than I left the store, my cell phone rang. I exhaled, hoping it was just the relief I was looking for.

It was Alice again.

"Hello."

"Payton, it's me."

"Did you hear anything?"

"No, I didn't. However, they just showed the front of the home on the news. I'm confident the pickup truck is the same color as Cole's. It's sitting in the front driveway."

"Oh, no."

"Look, there's nothing like being there in person instead of speculating, but the camera zoomed in pretty close. I tried to call the police station to see if they could confirm anything, but names aren't being released at the moment."

"Alright, Alice. I'm in the car now. I'll try to get there as fast as possible and call you back when I have information."

"Okay. Be careful, Payton."

I drove as fast as I could on a two-lane road heading to the most northern point of Pelican Beach. Even if I didn't have an exact address I could at least find the gated community. When I arrived, the sign for Forest Hill Estates couldn't be missed. It was a private golf club area within Pelican Beach, where only those with extra deep pockets occupied real estate.

At the front gate, I stopped the car and was greeted by a police officer.

"Good afternoon, officer."

"Good afternoon, ma'am. Are you a resident or family member to someone in Forest Hill Estates?"

"No, sir."

"Well, if that's the case, I'm going to have to ask you to turn your car around. We're currently dealing with an emergency," he said.

"Sir, I came here because I believe my fiance is involved in the fire. His renovation company was supposed to be doing a job in the area, and his mother called me worried because she thinks she saw his truck on the news."

"Ma'am, can you confirm the address where your fiance is working?"

"I can't. But I promise I wouldn't drive from the southern end of Pelican Beach if I didn't have good reason to believe he might be here."

The officer looked around for a minute as if he were contemplating what to do.

"Can you describe his truck?"

"Yes, it's black with a crew cab and tons of work materials in the back."

"Why don't you pull over to the side and let me radio to my partner in the back."

"Thank you."

The gates were opened, so I pulled over to the right and out of the way of traffic. I watched the officer in my side mirror, trying desperately to interpret what he was saying. Before I could make much of it, he started heading toward my side of the car.

"Okay, here's what you're going to do. I need you to pull in the gates and park right in front of the house to your right. Once the car is secure, you'll need to walk around the corner to the next row of houses. They have the yellow tape up, but my partner will be looking for you so he can help you confirm whether it's your fiance's truck."

"Okay." My voice was rattled. I knew there had to be some similarities with my description for him to allow me to get closer to the scene.

"Ma'am. What's your name?"

"Payton Matthews."

"Okay, Miss Matthews. Whatever you do, please adhere to the guidelines and stay behind the tape. Like I said, my officer will be looking for you."

"Okay, thank you."

I walked as fast as I could around the corner to the second street of homes. Just as they described on the radio, you could immediately see a lot of smoke coming from the house. With all the fire trucks blocking the way, I couldn't see the driveway, but I could see a big crane elevated to the top windows.

The officer came across the tape and walked toward me.

"Are you Payton Matthews?"

"Yes."

"I'm Officer Blackwell. I want you to stick with me. We're not going beyond the tape, but we can follow along the side where you should be able to see the vehicle you were describing to my partner."

"Okay."

I followed him several feet closer to the house. He turned to ask me another question.

"What's your fiance's name?"

"Cole Miller. He's the owner of Miller Renovations."

No sooner than I finished answering his question, I could see Cole's pickup parked in the driveway.

"Ma'am?... Ma'am?"

The officer was talking, but I couldn't tell you what he was saying. All I could hear were the emergency vehicles' engines as I tried to grasp the officer's arm and catch my breath.

PAYTON

"Mom... Mom... I'm fine. We're about to leave the hospital in a matter of minutes. I'm just waiting for my crutches, and then Payton is going to bring me home." Cole pleaded with his mother to remain calm. I knew the last thing he wanted was for her or Emmie to be frightened.

After spending a few more minutes on the phone, he hung up, looking worn out.

"What a day."

"What a day is right! Don't be too hard on your mother when you get home. I can only imagine how she must've felt when she saw your truck on the news."

"I don't doubt that she was scared."

He tried to adjust himself to a more comfortable position, but the pain caused him to grab his leg and gasp.

"If all I had to endure was a broken leg and a few bruises to get out of a house fire, then I really shouldn't complain."

I massaged his shoulders to try and help him relax. The more we listened to beeping machines and watched the staff walk back and forth, the more we were both ready to go home.

"Do you have any idea how the fire got started?"

"No. John, Miguel, and I were walking around the attic space trying to devise a plan for building the additional room upstairs."

"Doesn't that house already have a million rooms in it?"

"It does, but you know how some of the high-end clients can be. The more, the better."

He proceeded with the story.

"Anyway, at first, I thought I smelled something, but the odor was rather faint. We just assumed maybe somebody had burned something in the kitchen, and we didn't think much of it. As the odor started to intensify, I told the guys we better head downstairs and see what was going on. We made it out of the attic and no further than the stairwell before seeing dark smoke and flames at the bottom of the staircase."

"Gosh. That's terrible. I'm so glad you made it out safe. Was anyone else home?"

"Just their teenage boys and I believe a friend of theirs, but I can't be sure. It's not uncommon that we get access to the house when clients aren't home. I know for sure that my guys didn't have anything to do with whatever started the fire. We were all trapped together upstairs."

"Hopefully, one of the sons will have an explanation for what happened."

The nurse returned with Cole's crutches.

"Is this your first time using crutches?" she said.

"I've had my fair share of broken and fractured bones coming up as a young boy. I'm sure it will all come back to me just like second nature."

"Well, alright. I'll let the lovely lady hold your prescription while you get situated. You're going to want to fill this right away to help with the pain relief. I have a wheelchair to make it easier to get to your car."

"Thank you, ma'am, but I'm alright. I might as well go ahead and get reacquainted with the crutches."

Cole's first few steps were hard to watch, but he quickly found his cadence as he made his way down the hall and to the waiting room.

"How about you have a seat while I pull up the car?"

"I think I'd rather lean on my good leg and that wall over there. I don't think I can take too much getting up and down again."

"Are you sure? We should've taken the wheelchair that she offered."

"I'm fine. I'll be waiting right here when you get back."

"Okay."

I knew he was in an awful lot of pain, but his pride wouldn't let him admit it. I just hoped this wasn't the sign of a stubborn patient in the making.

On the ride home, he continued to tell me more about the fire.

"So how did Miguel end up being the only one remaining in the house and needing a crane to come to his rescue?"

"He was afraid to jump. John and I managed to jump down from one angle of the roof to another. After that, we just made the final jump. Our adrenaline must've been pumping because broken leg and all, I kept yelling at Miguel to jump, but he wouldn't."

"Wow, that's crazy."

"I know."

"After it's all over, you end up with a broken leg, John with a broken arm, and Miguel is fine."

"I'm glad he's fine. But, there was no way I was going to wait for those flames to finish making its way upstairs. I'm not sure what ignited it, but the heat felt intense."

"I don't blame you, babe. I'm just happy you're safe and

sound. We can always help you hobble down the aisle in July if need be."

"Haha. Thankfully, the cast should be off by then. How did you hear about the fire?"

"Natalie and I passed by a few sirens when we were returning from a photoshoot. But, it wasn't until a client came in the store and mentioned something about it that made me turn on the radio and listen. By then, I called your mom, and after she told me about what she heard on the news, that was my cue to come and check things out. Cole, I never felt more frightened than when I saw your truck in their driveway."

"Payton, I'm so sorry. The last thing I ever want to do is frighten you."

"It's not your fault."

He bit his lip as he tried to adjust his leg in the car. I hated to see him in pain, but I admired his bravery. He was a man made of steel when he needed to be and velvet when I needed it most.

At the house, Cole's mother, Alice, and Emmie came outside to give him a hand.

"Dad, are you okay?" Emmie said.

"Yes, Emms. Just in a little pain, that's all."

I whispered to Alice, "Don't let him fool you. I think he's in a lot more pain than he's letting on, but his medicine should help as soon as I go fill the prescription."

"I hear you two over there," Cole said.

"Aww, Cole, we don't want to see you in pain, that's all. There's some homemade soup on the stove for you, and Emmie made sure your bed has plenty of extra pillows so you can be comfortable." Having Alice around to take care of them was a Godsend.

"Thanks, but you already spoil me enough as it is. Don't go upping the anty. I'll figure things out and find a groove."

We ignored him and took turns, helping him to the living room and making sure he was comfortable. He removed his button-down shirt and wore only his shorts and his white undershirt to feel more relaxed. There was something about Cole that made even an undershirt look sexy.

"Poor guy..." I said as I adjusted the last pillow.

"I should get going, so I can turn in your prescription. I'm also going to call Natalie and have her lock up the store."

He pulled me by the belt loop on my shorts.

"Not before you plant one right here," Cole whispered while pointing to his lips.

Even amid pain, he still managed to find time for affection. For a brief moment, we snuck in a kiss. I was thankful the situation didn't turn out worse than it was.

Back in the car, I gave Natalie a call.

"Natalie, thank you sooo much. I don't know what I would've done without you today."

"No problem, I've got your back."

"I appreciate it, but I am definitely going to be paying you overtime. You didn't even get to eat lunch today, did you?"

"I had plenty of snacks to hold me over. Payton, seriously, do not worry about it. These things don't happen every day."

"You're the best. If you wouldn't mind switching the front sign to 'closed' and locking the door on your way out, that would be great. I'll swing by and take care of everything else later on."

"Okay, sounds good."

"Hey, Natalie."

"Yes?"

"Again... thank you."

At the pharmacy, I had to wait for what seemed like an eternity. I called my parents to check on them and give them an update.

"Hey, Mom."

"Hi, Payton. Boy, you're working pretty late this evening. I have a plate of food set aside for you."

"Thanks, I appreciate it. Today was definitely anything but ordinary."

"What happened?"

"The short version. I'm waiting at the pharmacy for Cole's pain medication because he was involved in a fire at his work site. He's home, and he's going to be fine, but he did break his leg and scuff himself up a bit."

"Was it the same fire in Forest Hills?" she said.

"That's the one."

"Oh, dear. I caught it on the news. I'm so glad he's okay. From the looks of things, I'm surprised the house is still standing."

"Thankfully, Cole and his crew made it out safe. He's a trooper for sure."

"Man, oh, man."

"How's Dad doing?" I asked.

"Today was another quiet day for the most part. He answered a few questions at his doctor's appointment but hasn't said much since he's been home."

"Did you tell the doctor there's been a shift in his demeanor?"

"I did, and he said it's not uncommon for people with dementia to become quiet or withdrawn. Payton, it just breaks my heart. I miss Will. I just want him to return to his old self. I'd almost rather him fuss at me for making his sweet tea bland, than to have him sit around here so quiet."

"I know, Mom."

She was quiet on the other end of the line. I tried to change the subject to uplift her spirit.

"Have you heard from Rebecca or Abby today?"

"I didn't speak to Abby, but Rebecca is about to lose her

mind on bed rest. Nobody knows what to do for her these days. She has fresh hot meals being delivered to the house daily. She even hired one of the girls from the spa to come and give her a massage."

"Seriously?"

I don't know why I was surprised. Rebecca always had a reputation for being high maintenance.

"Well, who am I to judge? I've never been pregnant a day in my life. If that's what will make her comfortable, then so be it."

I could hear the lady behind the desk calling my name for Cole's prescription.

"Mom, they're calling my name. I have to go. I should be home soon, okay?"

"Okay, dear. Be careful."

Later that evening, I tied up all of the day's loose ends and made my way home. A shower never felt so good. I was thankful for the time spent living at my parents' house. It helped me get back on my feet. But, with every passing month, as it got closer to the wedding, I started feeling like it was time to be with Cole.

I laid in bed, thinking about our future plans and was startled when the cell phone rang.

"Rebecca?" I answered.

"Yep, it's showtime."

"What?"

"You heard me," she said in between calculated breathing.

"We're in the car heading to the hospital. The baby is on the way. Tell everyone to meet us there," she said.

"Oh, my gosh. The baby is coming. Okay, I'm on it!"

I hung up before she could say anything else.

"Unbelievable."

This day was proving itself to be an extra dose of crazy. I took a deep breath and called my oldest sister, Abby.

"Hello?" She barely whispered into the phone.

"Hey Abs, it's Payton."

"Payton?"

"Yes."

"Good grief, what time is it?"

"Oh, it's late. It's about eleven o'clock, and Rebecca is in labor."

"Noooo. Right now?" She still sounded raspy.

"Well, it's not like the girl has a choice, Abby."

"Okay. Let me get myself together, and I'll meet you at the hospital."

"See you there." I hung up.

REBECCA

Hearing my baby boy cry for the first time brought tears of joy to my eyes. I don't know who cried more, me or my husband, Ethan. This past year had been a whirlwind for us. We were just two old high school sweethearts who reunited after years of being apart. It didn't take long for us to confess our renewed love. After a surprise pregnancy and a private wedding ceremony to follow, here we were welcoming our baby into the world.

"Welcome to the family, John William." Ethan rubbed our son's little arm. He was such a proud dad.

"Isn't he precious?" I said.

"He is. It seems like every time he hears your voice, he raises his eyebrows in response."

"Ethan, I'm so in love. John William is the most precious gift I've ever received."

"That makes two of us."

The doctor and nurses finished up and took us back to the room. I knew my family was itching to get in to meet the baby.

"Aww, there he is. My precious little grandson." Mom was so proud. Dad followed behind her with a big smile on his face.

"William, grab the hand sanitizer, honey."

Ethan exchanged congratulatory hugs with my parents. "Is everyone else in the waiting area?" he asked.

"You better believe it. Your parents are waiting, and so is Payton and Abby," mom said.

She turned back and admired John William from head to toe.

"Would you like to hold him?" I asked.

"Would I like to hold him? Gram didn't get up in the middle of the night just to come and say hello. Come here, little fella."

You would've thought this was my mother's first grandchild. She was elated, and even though dad wasn't as vocal, you could tell his heart was full by the look on his face.

"I'm sure Abby will fill you in when she comes in the room, but Wyatt sends his love. He stayed back at the house with the kids, of course."

"Oh, that's sweet. I feel terrible for interrupting everybody's sleep, but this little guy didn't want to wait until the morning."

Mom cooed over John William as he slept in her arms. "Look at my precious little grandbaby. We were ready to welcome you no matter what time you arrived."

"You guys would've lost it if you were with us during the car ride to the hospital. At one point, I literally thought I was going to deliver him in the car without an epidural."

"Wow. Did you have time to get the epidural once you arrived?"

"Barely. John William was ready to make a grand entrance. I guess he was just as tired of being in my belly as I was of having him there."

Mom thought that was funny, but it was true. I felt like I was ready to pop.

"Well, you must be operating in overdrive. Not only is it late, but you just gave birth. You need your rest."

I looked up and saw Ethan leading my sisters and my in-laws into the room.

"I know we're breaking all kinds of hospital rules. But everyone wants to say a quick hello, and then they're going to head home," Ethan said.

One after the other, everyone patiently waited their turn to get their first glimpse of John William. He didn't know it yet, but this baby was about to be spoiled with all the love and affection a family could offer.

"My youngest sister is a momma now." Abby had tears in her eyes. This was probably the closest we had been in a long while.

Both of my sisters fussed over me when the Davises took turns holding our sweet boy.

"I bet you're exhausted, aren't you?" Payton asked.

"It hasn't hit me yet with all the excitement. But trust me, as soon as we get a quiet moment, I'll probably knock right out."

“Ha! That’s funny. Hate to break it to ya, but you're in a hospital. There's no such thing as a quiet moment in a place like this. Trust me. This is my second trip to one today.” Payton had a good point. I never met anyone who left a hospital feeling well rested.

“Mom told me about Cole's accident earlier today. How's he doing?"

"According to him, it's just another broken bone. He seems to think the healing process shouldn't be a big deal. ‘I'll be fine, just like I was when I was younger’ he says.”

"Uh, the only problem is he's not a little kid anymore, he's in his forties. Children are way more resilient than adults."

"I tried to tell him, but I think he'll have to come to terms with it on his own." Payton shrugged.

"Take it from me, ladies, if you haven't learned this by now, you'll learn soon enough. Men can be very... very... stubborn. Especially when they're sick. Isn't that right, Arthur?"

I've always loved Dorothy. She's more of a no-nonsense, tell it like it is kind of woman, which is right up my alley.

"Excuse me?" Ethan's father teased.

"What on earth would make you say a thing like that, Dorothy?" He smirked at her, but I think everybody knew better.

"Don't play innocent with me, Arthur. Ethan has witnessed your stubbornness firsthand, haven't you?"

"I'm staying out of this one." Ethan put his hands up in surrender.

Everyone fussed over the baby for a little while longer.

"Alright, y'all. You know I love you, and I'm hoping I'll see every last one of you at the house for diaper changing, feedings, and everything in between. But unless you're sticking around for breastfeeding 101..."

"Say no more, Miss Rebecca. I was just coming to tell your guests they'll have to return during visiting hours." Nurse Jones didn't play around.

When I arrived, she had everyone hopping at the snap of a finger to make way for my delivery.

Everyone said their goodbyes. By sunrise the next day, I was just as exhausted as ever. The only thing I wanted to do was curl up in my own bed and retreat for a little while.

"Can I get anything for you?" Ethan offered.

"A good night's rest might be nice. Other than that, I'm good."

"I'm sorry, Becca. You barely had a chance to sleep last night. You must be tired."

"I might as well get used to it. Sleepless nights may be the new routine for a while to come. You, on the other hand, snored and purred like a kitten as usual."

He thought it was funny, but I didn't. I contemplated what it would be like to whack him with a pillow and play dumb after.

"I'm not sure about the snoring, but my body feels like it was hit by a Mack truck."

"Ethan, don't talk to me about how your body feels right now. Would you like to trade positions? Try pushing a whole baby out of you, then we can talk."

"There she is! There's my sugar and spice."

He hopped up on the bed and laid beside me while we waited for the nurse to bring John William back.

"I was wondering how long it would take for that fiery personality of yours to come back out. I was starting to think the baby was turning you into mush," he said.

"Is being fiery a bad thing?"

"Absolutely not. I mean it in the best way possible. I've always loved that about you. All that spice is what drew me in and caused me to fall in love with you all over again."

I felt myself starting to tear up a bit, but I didn't let it show.

"Good, because if you told me it was a bad thing, I would've knocked you into next week."

Ethan knows I have just enough crazy in me to do it.

"Well, if that's the case, I'll be sure to stay on your good side. Besides, I don't want to mess up an opportunity to come back here next year for baby number two."

My eye rolling abilities were on full display at this point.

"Baby number two? Our son hasn't been here twenty-four hours yet, and you're already talking about baby number two? Don't hold your breath on that one. As a matter of fact, if you need to sleep in the guest room, you let me know."

"Only if you're sleeping in the guest room with me. Maybe we can try for twins the next time. We can have a whole girl scout troop or baseball team. Maybe even a little of both."

Thankfully, I knew Ethan was egging me on. He always loved to get me all wound up.

Nurse Jones interrupted our little charade.

"Is everything okay in here? I could practically hear you two down the hall."

"Everything's fine. It was just my husband in here acting like a clown."

"Well, make sure you save all of that extra energy for when you go home tomorrow. In the meantime, I need to perform a routine check on Miss Rebecca."

The thought of going home tomorrow was bittersweet. I wanted to get adjusted to our new life with John William, but I was also a little nervous.

"Sir, if you don't mind, I'll have to ask you to get out of the bed. You'll have plenty of time to snuggle with your wife when she's ready to have baby number two."

Ethan and I looked at each other. We all laughed so hard. Clearly, we were pretty loud if she could repeat that.

"Just kidding. That's between you and the man upstairs," she said.

The nurse began to pull the curtain closed. Ethan took his cue to leave and get something to eat. While she was poking and probing, I could hear my cell phone buzzing away.

"I bet you have folks lined up and ready to meet that handsome boy of yours," she said.

"Now that the word is out, I bet you're right. Thanks for the compliment, by the way."

"You're welcome. Whatever you do, don't feel pressured to cater to everyone's schedule. There will be plenty of time for visitors."

"I can't argue with you there. Can I ask you a question?" I said.

"Ask as many questions as you want."

"Is it normal for me to be feeling a little anxious about going home?"

"It's very normal. A lot of first-time mothers put pressure on themselves to have it all together. Some feel defeated before they even leave the hospital. The key is to give yourself permission to make mistakes. No one expects you to be the perfect mother. Not even your baby boy."

"Yeah, maybe that's what it is. I think I'm starting to realize that I based all of my success on my career and climbing up the ladder. I'm good at being a lawyer. Darn good if I may say so myself. But motherhood is completely different. My sister Abby is a natural. I'm still learning how to be a wife, so you can only imagine how I feel."

"Did you learn how to become a good lawyer overnight?"

"No."

"Well, then you understand exactly where I'm going with this."

"Yes, ma'am. I sure do."

"I'm not married, but I would imagine the same applies to learning how to become a good wife."

When she was finished, she pulled the curtain back and revealed a beautiful view of downtown. I could see the shores of Pelican Beach in the distance, which made me long to close my eyes and lay beneath the sun.

PAYTON

Cole was conducting most of his work from home for the next six to eight weeks. Since he normally liked to get his hands dirty, Alice and I were praying he didn't drive everyone crazy.

"Payton, I've been thinking," he said.

"Uh oh. Should I be nervous?"

"Nervous about what? This is a fun idea."

"Okay."

"Since you're all going shopping for your wedding dress today, I thought I'd give you something to consider. Of course, the ultimate decision is still yours."

"Mmm hmm."

"Since we're having such a hard time narrowing down a place for the ceremony, I was wondering if you'd like to revisit the idea of getting married right here on the beach?"

You could barely hear a pin drop in the room. Even mom and Emmie stopped to give the topic their full attention.

"Again. It's no pressure. I just want whatever will make you happy."

"You know Payton, that might not be a bad idea. So far, it's the least expensive, most romantic, and the most intimate option by far," mom said.

"I don't doubt for one minute that it would be nice, but I really had my heart set on Marina Del Mar. Their event planner asked me to wait another day to see if she could make arrangements to squeeze us in for July. Wouldn't you want to at least hear what she has to say?"

"Sure. I want whatever you want. It was just an option," Cole said.

Emmie sketched in her notebook while Alice grabbed her keys off the table.

"Why the long faces? It's time to perk up and go shopping for a wedding dress!"

"No long faces. We were just trying to tackle the never ending saga of where to have the wedding. It's kind of strange that I'm going to pick out my dress and still don't have the venue secured."

"Oh, honey, stop being so hard on yourself. You had no way of knowing that most of your favorite venues in Pelican Beach wouldn't be able to accommodate you because of a convention. Since when do we ever have conventions out here anyway?" Mom was just as frustrated as I was.

"Payton, have you considered pushing the wedding to August or September? That might give you a little more flexibility." Alice was right, but I didn't want to belabor the wedding any longer.

Cole shook his head in disagreement.

"Even I don't want to do that. I'm ready to have my wife come join me and Emmie here at the beach house for good. We've waited long enough. Right, Emms?"

Emmie had plugged in her ear pods while drawing and didn't hear a word of what he was saying.

"Cole's right. We've done this the traditional way and waited to move in together. But, it's time. And come hell or high water I have one goal to accomplish before the end of July, and that's to become Mrs. Cole Miller."

Cole always thought it was attractive whenever I talked about becoming his Mrs.

"Aren't they cute together?" Mom looked at Alice who entered the room. The two mothers had formed a nice bond over time.

"They sure are."

"When I grow up I want a relationship just like theirs." Alice threw her purse over her shoulder.

"Speaking of relationships, how's things with the gentleman from your neighborhood?" I asked.

Mom interrupted. "Well, wait a minute. I know it's been a while since we've had a chance to catch up, but I didn't realize you were in a relationship, Alice."

"Helen, it's no big deal. Besides, today is all about Payton. Now everybody grab your things and let's go." She put on her wide framed sunglasses and started heading for the door.

"Oh, no you don't. I can detect avoidance coming a mile away."

"I have no idea what you're talking about, Payton."

I knew better but I let it slide until we got to the car.

"Cole, are you sure you're going to be okay here all by yourself? Emmie can always stay if you need company."

"I'll be fine. I have the phone right beside me should anything come up."

"Okay. Come on, Emmie. We're leaving."

Forgetting that she couldn't hear us I waved my hands around to get her attention.

In the car, we continued to probe Alice until she told us everything about her friend.

"Alice, you know we're not going to be able to carry on with the day until we hear about your guy friend, right?"

"I don't know that there's much to tell. His name is Stanley. I met him at one of my neighborhood HOA meetings. He's a little older than I am but keeps himself up very nice. He attributes his walking routine to his good health and he's a self proclaimed paddle ball champion. I'll have to take his word for it because I've never seen him play. Finally, he's reliable."

"Uh oh." Mom put on her shades and looked out the window.

"What?" Alice said.

"You used the word reliable to describe someone you're seeing. That can't be good."

I quickly glanced at Alice in the rear view mirror.

"I'm going to have to agree with mom on this one. I mean, it's nice that he's reliable and all. But, he doesn't sound like he's the right fit if all you can come up with is 'well put together and reliable.'"

"What's wrong with being reliable? My late husband, Bill was the most reliable man I knew outside of my father, God rest his soul."

"But I'm sure you didn't fall in love with Bill because of his reliability," mom said.

Alice was quiet for a moment before breaking her silence.

"I guess not."

"All that matters is that you're happy, Alice." I checked the rear view again but she seemed to have drifted off into her own thoughts.

"Stanley has been a nice companion. I wouldn't even say that we're officially dating. At least, if he's interested he's never said anything. But, I can always count on him to bring my favorite Chamomile tea with a small slice of pound cake and to come around and keep me company. I really don't have anything bad to say about him but..."

I knew I could feel a 'but' coming on. Emmie was dozing in the back, and I turned down the radio so that I wouldn't miss a word.

"Even though he's a nice man, someone else has my attention as a potential love interest."

By now I had pulled into a parking space and was able to turn around and listen.

"I've met someone who makes me feel alive."

Mom slapped the dashboard.

"That's what I'm talking about. Now we're cooking with gas!"

We laughed so loud until Emmie woke up and I almost tinkled.

"Seriously? Who says that?"

"Well, it's the truth. Who wants to spend the rest of their life with an old reliable prune? Again, not to say that reliable isn't good. But if the other man knows how to light your fire, then what's the problem?"

"Who's lighting a fire?" Emmie said in her sleepy voice.

The laughter spiraled out of control all over again.

"No one is lighting a fire, Emmie. We're just being silly, that's all."

"Mm hmm," mom said.

"Ladies, we'll have to continue this conversation later. Right now, it's time for my future daughter-in-law to find a wedding dress. Come on, Emmie. Let's go!"

Mom and I followed behind them.

"I'm just so sorry your sisters couldn't be here, Payton."

"I know but we all felt much better with Abby staying back to look after dad. And, Rebecca is house bound with the baby, so it only made sense."

"Well, the good news is you'll have them by your side on your special day."

Seeing all the dresses on display took me back to the first time I was getting married. Back then I had to have the longest train imaginable and was obsessed with the royal look. This time I wanted something a lot more simple.

~

"Welcome to Bridal Elegance. My name is Darla. How may I help you?"

"Hi. I'm Payton Matthews and this is my mother Helen, this is Alice, and this sweet young lady is Emmie. We're all here for my 10:00 appointment to try on dresses."

"Perfect. I'll be assisting you today."

Darla was petite with a welcoming smile. She led us back to an area where everyone could sit while I tried on dresses.

"Ladies, you can make yourself comfortable. Before we get started with trying on dresses can I offer you something to drink?"

"I'm good, thank you." I checked with the others but they were fine as well.

"Okay. Payton, I'll need to get a feel for what you're looking for before we get started."

"Sure."

"For starters, where are you having your wedding?"

I felt embarrassed that I still didn't know.

"That's still in the air. It could be at Marina Del Mar or ..."

I turned and looked at my support team sitting over on the couch.

"It could be on the beach. I guess I need to look at dresses that could be fitting for both places."

"That's not a problem at all. With today's modern styles there should be plenty to choose from."

Then she leaned in closer.

"You're not the first bride to be undecided about your venue. Don't worry. Everything will be just fine."

"Thank you."

"Okay, back on track. Do you have a particular style in mind? We have mermaid dresses, even though that might be a bit challenging on the beach. Then there's the A-line, trumpet, sweetheart neckline, strapless?"

"Maybe something with cap sleeves so I don't have to constantly fidget with the dress. Also, I'd love to see some detail on the back. I don't have a particular neckline in mind but I want an overall romantic look."

"Okay. I'm going to get started on pulling a few dresses for your fitting room. Oh, one more thing before I forget. What's your budget?"

I could hear Mom commenting in the background.

"Spare no expenses. She deserves the best!"

I wouldn't dare expect my family to contribute to our wedding expenses. They already paid for one wedding, and I'm sure they've already spent more than their fair share to help prepare for John William.

"Mom is sweet, but I actually do want to stick to a budget. My fiancé gave me a blank check and said I could make it out for this amount..."

I showed her a note with a healthy sized figure on it.

"However, I'd like to lean on the conservative side and spend half of that amount or even less if we can help it," I said.

"You have a very generous fiancé."

"I do. But I'd much rather see the funds go toward something for our future."

"I know exactly what you mean. So basically we need to find a gorgeous wedding dress that looks like it cost the entire budget but is a steal of a deal."

"Darla, I knew I liked you from the moment you greeted us at the front door."

She really was nice and made me feel at ease.

"Likewise. Now let's find your wedding dress."

About an hour into the appointment I had tried on several dresses but none of them seemed to do it for me. Even my cheering squad was starting to grow less enthusiastic.

"Hang in there, Payton. I'm certain there's a dress here with your name on it," Alice said.

Emmie was wandering around the store looking at dresses and entertaining herself. She pulled out one in particular that looked like it was fit for a princess.

"Payton, I bet you'd look pretty in this one," she said.

Darla walked over and took the dress off the hook. It did look pretty from afar but so did the others until I tried them on.

"What do you think, Payton? It's priced right and it's your size. Would you like to try this one on?"

"Sure. Emmie, I hope you picked a winner because this is the last one I'm trying on for today."

I retreated to the back and slipped into the last dress for the day. I watched in the mirror as Darla helped me put the dress on. The neckline had lace over organza to give an illusion of sheerness. The bottom was a soft cotton A-line.

"Turn around so you can see the back," Darla said.

The details from the front carried over and framed an open keyhole. The dress was absolutely stunning.

"You have a glow about you that's undeniable. But what do you think about the dress?"

I turned back to the mirror.

"I love it!"

"You do?"

"Yes, it's perfect in every way. It has an elegant Boho vibe that's perfect for the beach!"

I placed both hands over my mouth.

"What about Marina Del Mar?" Darla asked.

"Honestly, I think the moment I put this dress on it all became clear. Who needs Marina Del Mar when we can have a romantic wedding on the beach?"

Of course, Cole knew this all along. But, sometimes I needed a personal experience before I could arrive at the same conclusion.

"Wait. Before we get ahead ourselves let's see what everyone else thinks," I said.

"Not before I give you this..."

She placed a jeweled tiara with a veil on to add the finishing touch. I wanted to wait until I was outside but I could already feel my emotions getting the best of me.

"Ohhh, Payton. This is the dress, isn't it?"

I could only nod my head as I tried to pat my eyes dry.

"You see..."

I continued to speak in between sniffles.

"The thing is. After everything my ex-husband put me through I didn't think I had it in me to love again. And now look at me, standing here in this dress. I'm so amazed. There are no words to describe how good it makes me feel. No words."

"Wow, keep it up and you're going to make me cry. There's just something about hearing a love story that gets me every time," Darla said.

"Oh, dear. You work here so I can only imagine how many tissues you go through every day!"

Now that my face was all red I knew I had to pull myself

together. Darla led me out to the showroom to show off my wedding dress to my family.

"Well, what do you think?"

Darla fluffed the back of the dress and made sure the veil was just so. Mom immediately raised her hands to her cheeks and Alice started clapping.

"I think you look like a beautiful princess," Emmie said.

"Thank you, Emmie. And, I owe it all to you."

She beamed at the idea of being the one who found my dress.

"Mom? Alice?"

I could tell they liked it, but I needed to hear their words of confirmation.

"What's not to like, Payton? It's like Emmie said. You look beautiful," Alice said.

Mom stood up and came closer.

"Stunning. Absolutely stunning. And, if you ask me, it's perfect for a beach wedding."

Darla was drying the corner of her eyes.

"Your mother knows you well, Payton," she said.

"She sure does!"

"So, do I hear you saying that you want to have a beach wedding, and you're taking this dress home with you today?"

I paused and then belted out, "Yes!!"

Everyone was so happy. Even a few of the customers in the store stopped to cheer us on.

"Emmie, I owe you big time."

We were so excited we danced and twirled around one another.

"You saved the day. I was starting to feel defeated until you found this dress."

"Payton, we may have a fashion consultant in our midst," mom said.

Emmie shrugged her shoulders. "Maybe it was just good luck."

"Well, either way, I'm grateful."

I could envision the look on Cole's face when we told him the news. A beach wedding was so appropriate for us. I don't know why I didn't see it right from the start. We both had traditional weddings the first time around. This would be something new and special. Something we could call our own.

I was still bubbling over with joy in the car.

"I just want to thank everyone for coming with me today. Emmie, you deserve an extra big thanks for helping me find my dress."

Emmie already had her ear buds back in so Alice had to get her attention.

"Yes, Grandma?"

"Payton said thank you for helping her find her wedding dress."

"Oh, you're welcome, Payton."

She leaned forward and gave me a big thumbs up before returning to her music.

"Kids today have so much technology, I don't know how they can keep up with it all, " Alice said.

"Isn't that the truth. When I was a little girl we enjoyed playing hopscotch and riding our bikes. Today, it seems like kids prefer staying glued to their devices," I said.

Mom nodded. "The kids and adults for that matter. I guess it's just the times we're living in."

I thought it was a good time to shift back to Alice's love interest.

"So, Alice. I'm dying to hear the rest of your story about your new friend ... what's his name again?"

"I don't think I mentioned his name. Besides, I'm sure you'd rather hear about something more interesting, Payton."

"More interesting? Nonsense. What could be more interesting than hearing about somebody else's love life!"

"Love life! Both of them are just friends, that's all," Alice said.

Mom turned around.

"Yeah, right! Come on, Alice. Come clean," she said.

"Alright. But you have to promise not to say anything, Payton, especially not to Cole. He always makes a big fuss over my love life and I never understand why."

"Scout's honor. He won't hear a peep from me."

"Helen, you, too."

"Yes, me, too... Scout's honor."

"Okay. I have a habit of going to the bookstore at least once a week. I usually peruse my favorite sections and take a stack of books with me to sit and read in the cafe. I can stay in there for hours with a cup of tea and a good book."

"Mmm hmm." I was anxious for her to get to the good part.

"Well, one particular Saturday I noticed a gentleman sitting nearby reading. He smiled at me. Of course, I didn't think much of it. He seemed friendly enough but then we both returned back to our reading. For the next two months or better the same thing would happen over and over again. I missed a few Saturdays here and there, but whenever I went he was there."

"A whole two months?" mom asked.

"It sounds like a long time just to smile and notice somebody. But we were both strangers so I was perfectly okay with it. I started looking forward to seeing if he was going to be there. It became like a fun little game to glance over to the spot where he normally sits without being too obvious. I would look, and say to myself 'yep, he's here' and then get my books and carry on with my usual routine. Until one day that all changed. One day I could see him getting up and walking toward me out of the corner of my eye. I remember thinking, 'nooo, he's not coming to my table.' And, then I thought, 'oh, yes, he is coming to my table!' I pretended to be reading and then he said, 'hi, my name is Carl, do you mind if I join you?" Alice paused.

"What did you say?" I asked.

"I introduced myself and told him my name, and that's it. We've been seeing each other ever since."

Mom threw her hands in the air.

"That's it? You can't leave us hanging like that. I thought this was the man who knows how to light your ..."

"Mom!" I interjected.

"What? I wasn't going to say anything bad. I just know there's more to the story," she said.

"You're right, Helen. There is more. Carl has been my Saturday date ever since we met. In the beginning we used to just share the table space together. We'd have a little small talk here and there. I learned that he's a retired professor, he told me about his family and I reciprocated. As of late our conversations are even more invigorating. He even left me a single stem rose on my chair the first time he ever expressed interest."

The little kid in me came out while singing 'Alice has a boyfriend.'

I could see her grinning in the rear view mirror.

"Okay, we're almost at the house. Hurry up and tell us the good stuff. What does he look like? Have you kissed yet? We need details," mom said.

I don't know who was worse, me or my mother.

"I can't rush this story along. Trust me. You want to hear the whole thing in its proper sequence. It's the conclusion that has me in a state of not knowing what to do."

"Okay, well at least start with his looks. Is he good looking?"

Alice laughed.

"I think he is. He has white hair that's thinning at the top but he wears it well. He has a nice Floridian tan and stays in excellent shape. Oh, and he still dresses like a professor."

"A handsome professor who lives in the bookstore. Hmm." I was taking it all in.

"We've dined out, been to a couple of plays and even slow danced in my living room. But all of that recently came to a screeching halt."

"Why?" It was clear that Alice was into this guy so I wondered what the problem could be.

"Stanley found us kissing on my front porch earlier this week."

"Shut up!" Mom lost it.

"I'm sorry. Carry on," she said.

By now we had been sitting in front of the house for at least ten minutes. Emmie, as usual, was mesmerized by the car and fell asleep. And, Cole could've been in the house hobbling around for all we knew, but we were determined to hear the end of the story.

"So wait. What was Stanley doing there in the first place?" I asked.

As soon as the words came out of my mouth I remembered what Alice told us earlier.

"Thursday tea," we said in unison.

"It was my fault. Stanley was just coming by to bring my usual Chamomile tea and pound cake. It completely slipped my mind that it was his day to stop by. I felt terrible."

"Now I see why you refer to him as reliable. For goodness sake, it's okay to miss a Thursday every now and again," mom said.

She was clearly favoring Carl over Stanley.

"The worst part was the look on his face. The timing couldn't have been more awful."

"What happened next?"

Just then Cole called from the front door standing with his crutches.

"Are you guys alright out there?"

Sadly, his timing felt like an interruption right in the middle of a good movie. Emmie woke up and we all agreed to reconvene later to hear the rest of Alice's story.

PAYTON

The next day I planned a special date at the beach house with Cole. Emmie was enjoying a visit with one of her friends, and my intentions were to spoil Cole with some alone time for two.

"While I'd prefer not to have a broken leg, this accident has taught me how important it is to slow down and smell the roses," Cole said.

We sat under the pergola and listened to sound of the ocean. He put his arm around me.

"I agree. It's easy to get entangled in daily affairs and forget what matters most."

"Promise me that will never happen to us. Let's make it a priority to never get too caught up and let life pass us by." Cole looked deeply into my eyes.

"I can't promise that we'll always get it right, but I promise to always make you... to make us my priority," I said.

"That's all I could ever ask."

We ate the lunch that I prepared and continued taking in the beautiful view.

"You know, Cole. I think most of our dates have been right here at this house."

"It seems that way, but I promise that will change as soon as I can get this old leg back on track."

"There's nothing about your leg or you that's old."

"Thank you, but for some reason these bones don't feel the same way they did when I was twenty."

I could agree with that. Lately it felt like my bones creaked and popped in new places I had never experienced before.

"Hey, Payton."

"Yes."

"I just want to reassure you that although you changed your mind having the ceremony here on the beach, you don't have to. I don't want you to feel pressured into it. I'm thrilled that we had a chance to get engaged here. If Marina Del Mar is still your number one, then I fully support that, too."

"Cole, I promise I genuinely want to have the wedding here. I know sometimes it takes longer than a minute for me to come around to an idea, and I apologize for that. But just think of the memories we'll have here. You know we can never sell this house, right?"

Cole tilted his head back and let out a hardy laugh.

"Wow, you've definitely had a change of heart."

He drew my hand closer and held it with our fingers intertwined.

"You won't get any arguments out of me. I used to think that living full time in a beach house wasn't the norm until we moved to Pelican Beach. I always thought they were vacation homes or off season homes. I'd live here every day for the rest of my life if I could. And, to know that my lady feels the same way makes it even better."

I rested my head on his shoulder.

"So what do you have in mind for the wedding?" Cole asked.

"Picture this." I spread my hands out in the direction of the beach.

"What if we had an archway draped in white chiffon and flowers where we will exchange our vows? Rows and rows of chairs draped in white linen with bows tied around the back. Linen tablecloths with bouquets of flowers to serve as a centerpiece. Perhaps peonies or hydrangeas blooming in different shades of beige and pink. Of course, we'll have to come up with a solution for a dance floor. Maybe we can have the rental company set up an amazing outdoor tent. Oh, and let's not forget a live band and..."

"Whoa, whoa... slow down there. I can hardly keep up."

"You don't like my ideas?" I asked.

"Your ideas sound fantastic. It's been a while since I've seen you this excited about the wedding. I just wanted to slow down and savor the moment."

"Gee, was I that bad?"

"Not bad. I just think you've been under a lot of pressure as most brides are. And, when things weren't working out according to plan it probably made it worse. I can't say the same anymore. I'm convinced that having the wedding here was a good fit for you."

"It was a good fit for us. Honestly, I don't know what I would do without you in my life. You're so supportive, Cole. I love you."

"I love you, too."

"Why don't we continue talking about the plans later. You and I are on a date, remember?"

"I remember."

"Good. Since you're the one in a cast I think you deserve to be catered to and enjoy something special I planned for you."

"Oh, really? What did you have in mind?"

"Wouldn't you like to know?" I said in a flirtatious voice.

"Can I have a hint?"

"I'll give you more than a hint. Hold that thought. I'll be right back."

I ran to the car as fast as I could to get the surprise. On occasion I had a habit of stopping by a thrift store to collect vintage items for fun. The last time I found a coo-coo clock for the store. This week's find was sure to add some fun to our date.

I returned wheeling the object behind me and peeked outside at Cole.

"Are you ready?"

"Ready as I'll ever be."

"Okay, close your eyes, and don't open them until I say so."

I made sure everything was plugged in, turned on some background music, and asked Cole to open his eyes. He immediately laughed.

"A karaoke?" he asked.

Before he could say anything I started serenading him to the tune of one of his favorite songs. I didn't know all of the words but we didn't care. We sat around singing song after song off key. Thankfully, the neighbors weren't close enough to complain or call the police.

REBECCA

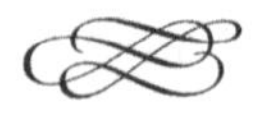

I was home for a couple of weeks with John William and felt like a complete zombie. Ethan and I were over the moon in love with our son, but our irregular sleeping habits were finally starting to take its toll.

Abby was coming over with my niece and nephew. I couldn't wait to talk to someone with more experience.

"Hi, Aunt Rebecca!" Maggie planted a sloppy kiss on my cheek.

"Hi, love. Ooh, I've missed those sweet kisses. How's my favorite niece doing?"

Abby followed her inside but I noticed Aidan was nowhere in sight.

"You say that all the time but I'm your only niece."

"Okay, you caught me. Hey, where's Aidan?"

"He had to stay home with daddy because he threw up today.

I poked out my bottom lip.

"Aww, that's too bad. I was looking forward to him meeting John William."

Abby gave me a bear hug.

"So was I but we decided not to take any chances. I'm sure it had something to do with him hanging upside down like a monkey after eating lunch. But, you can never be too careful with a newborn."

"Aunt Rebecca, what did you do with John William? I don't see him anywhere.

I loved Maggie's innocence. She seemed convinced that I was playing a game of hiding go seek with the baby.

"He's right over here in the living room. But first..."

"I know. I have to wash my hands. Mom already told me all the rules in the car. She said 'wash your hands, if you let me hold him I have to be sitting on the couch, and I have to put a pillow under his neck."

Maggie was so sweet. She was ready to meet her baby cousin and I certainly wasn't going to get in her way. Her mannerisms were very much like Abby's when it came to being nurturing.

"Alright kiddo, let's go wash our hands," Abby said.

When they returned I positioned John William on Maggie's lap.

"So, how are you feeling, Sis?"

"The truth? Happy, tired, moody... did I mention tired?"

"Rebecca, you recently gave birth. What did you expect?"

"I know what all of the books said I should expect but there's nothing like experiencing it for yourself."

"That's a good point."

"Ethan has been great about checking on me during late night feedings, but he can only do so much. I finally told him this afternoon to head upstairs and take a nap. He disappeared so fast it was hysterical. I'm sure he'll come down and say hello before you leave."

I glanced over at Maggie who was putting John William right to sleep. She was a natural.

"He's so precious, Aunt Rebecca. I already love him so much."

"Aww, aren't you sweet, Maggie."

"I don't know, Abby. I might have to steal my niece every now and again. I didn't realize we had a built in babysitter in the family."

"Oh, I'm sure she'd love that. Wouldn't you, Maggie?"

"Yep! Do you want to hold him, Mom?"

"Oh, you mean I get to have a turn? Why, yes thank you. I don't mind if I do." Abby teased.

It brought such joy to watch them connect with John William.

"Maggie, would you like to watch one of your favorite channels or play on your tablet while I catch up with Aunt Rebecca?"

Maggie ran off to turn the television on while John William continued to sleep in Abby's arms.

"Rebecca, it's really a beautiful thing to see you in your new role as a mother."

"Ha, thanks, but I still have a lot to learn."

"Don't be so tough on yourself. I know we've had our share of bumping heads in the past, but you should know that I'm here for you if you need anything."

"Thank you. I appreciate it. I think my biggest challenge is trying to find balance. We haven't been home that long and already issues are starting to pop up at work. And, we still have to find a property management company for the house in Savannah."

"Would you like some advice?"

"Sure."

"Try to be one hundred percent focused on your maternity

leave. The job will be there when you get back, and somebody else can make arrangements for renting the house."

I sighed.

"You're right."

"Just keep bonding with your sweet baby boy. He needs you."

A floodgate of tears let loose. Abby wasn't saying anything bad. I was just so used to trying to be superwoman. It didn't occur to me that I could be potentially focused on all the wrong things.

Abby gently placed John William in his bassinet.

"Come here and give your big sis a hug."

She held me for what seemed like an eternity and allowed me to cry out all of my exhaustion.

"Thank you. I needed that. I feel so much better."

"Oh, well, if that's all you needed to feel better I can come over and make you cry again tomorrow if you'd like."

I let out a good snort and found myself in the middle of a laughing spell.

"Listen, I have an idea. Maggie is well entertained and John William is napping. I feel like the biggest gift I could offer you is free time to get some rest. Go on up and join Ethan. John William will be fine."

"Oh, Abby, I couldn't. You came over here to visit with me."

"We have plenty of time to visit. These opportunities don't come along often. You better take advantage," she said.

"But..."

"Rebecca, as your oldest sister I won't take no for an answer, and I might put you over my knee if you don't quit arguing with me." Abby cleared her throat.

When we were little kids and I was being naughty, sometimes mom would send Abby after me. I remember it just like it was yesterday.

"Alright. I won't argue with you as long as you promise to wake me if I sleep past an hour."

"I will not. You sleep as long as you need to. Worse case scenario Ethan can take over when he gets up."

"Alright... are you sure?"

"Rebeccaaaa!"

"Okay, I'm gone."

I hugged Abby one last time then tip toed upstairs to take a much needed nap. Even though we spent most of our lives bumping heads growing up, I was thankful that we had finally bonded over motherhood, something we both held near and dear to our hearts.

ALICE

It was around noon on Thursday when the doorbell rang. I wasn't expecting Stanley this week. He hadn't spoken to me since he last saw me with Carl. Who could blame him? I felt like a fool for putting myself on public display, and even worse for breaking his heart.

"Stanley. I didn't think you were coming today."

He stood holding my usual cup of Chamomile tea with a slice of pound cake in a bag.

"I almost didn't. I can leave if you want me to."

"No, please come in."

He walked past me and laid everything down on the kitchen counter. Still standing with his back facing me he began to speak.

"I rehearsed everything I wanted to say a thousand times. Now that I'm here, I don't know where to begin."

"I know. I'm sorry, Stanley."

"Do you know? ... Do you know what it feels like to look up and see the woman you love entangled with another man?"

"I ... well, no. I guess I don't know what it's like to be on the receiving end of that. I do know that I never meant to hurt you."

There was nothing I could say in this moment that would ever be good enough. He turned around and faced me.

"Do you love him?" He hung his head low.

"I don't know. I'm still trying to figure it out."

"Well, I guess I have myself to blame for that. Here I thought we had something special. But clearly I wasn't enough for you."

"Stanley, I don't mean any harm, but up until today, I've never really known where you and I stood. Today was the first time I've ever heard you use the word love as it pertains to us."

He thought about it before he began speaking.

"Everyone has different strengths. I've never been a man of many words but I've always been here for you. I thought that meant something."

He started making his way back toward the foyer before turning around.

"Every time I walk through that door with your favorite tea I'm doing it because I love you. Every time I fix something for you I'm also demonstrating that you can count on me. That's my way of screaming from the mountain top that I love you. Sure... could I do a better job at being more forward about it? Clearly the answer is yes. But I don't know how you couldn't see love standing right here in front of you, Alice. I just don't get it."

I was crushed. He turned to leave and shared a few parting words on his way out the door.

"I'll give you time to think things through, Alice. But you should know that I'm not walking away without trying my best to win you over. Mr. Suave can't just swoop his way in and ruin what we have. Not unless you want him to."

Stanley closed the door behind him. I had to sit to keep from falling.

I tried taking it all in but the phone rang.

"Hello?"

"Good afternoon. Is this Ms. Alice Miller?"

"Yes, who is this?"

"This is Veronica calling from T&T Marketing. If you have a moment we'd love to talk to you to review your account and tell you about a few of our promotions."

"Thank you, but I'm not interested."

"I see. Ma'am, perhaps you'd like to take a moment to hear about the..."

I hung up the phone. May the good Lord forgive me, but the last person I need to hear from is another telemarketer during a time like this.

The phone rang again.

"Ma'am, I told you I'm not interested. And, I'd prefer that you'd kindly remove my number from your list please."

"Alice?"

"Carl?"

"Yes, it's me. Are you okay?"

"Oh, Carl. I'm sorry. I constantly receive calls from telemarketers. I guess I allowed the last one to get under my skin."

"Who can blame you? Marketing calls and robo calls can be frustrating. Perhaps I can cheer you up?" he said.

"That's sweet of you, Carl, but I'll be fine."

"I know you'll be fine, but I called because I feel like spoiling you this evening, if you're free?"

I hesitated for a moment. I barely had time to think about what just happened with Stanley. All I really wanted was a quiet evening alone.

"Carl, I don't know about this evening. I think I'm more in the mood for a quiet evening at home."

"Okay, a quiet evening at home it is. I'll bring supper to you. I'll bring your favorite bottle of wine. And, if you want I can stay quiet the whole time. It will be like I'm not even there."

"What's the point of coming if you're going to be quiet? You can't do that."

"I can do anything for you, Alice. Therefore, I'm coming and I won't take no for an answer. I can be there by six."

"Alright, I'll see you then."

I caved in. I really didn't want to spend the evening with anyone. I just wanted to sift through my quiet thoughts but my guilty conscious got the best of me. I never expected to be in my early seventies trying to decide between two men. Carl knew how to deliver the romance, but Stanley always makes me feel at home. I closed my eyes and drifted off for a little while.

~

It felt like an hour had passed before the doorbell rang.

"Carl?"

He stood on my porch holding several bags.

"You seem surprised. I told you I'd be here at six."

"You're fine. I closed my eyes to rest for a little while and must've fallen asleep longer than planned."

"That means you needed the rest. Where can I put everything?"

"Follow me. You can lay everything over here on the kitchen table. We can even eat in here if it's okay with you."

"It's fine with me."

"I need a minute to go freshen up and I'll be right back. Do you need anything from me first?"

"The restaurant set us up with utensils so I should be good."

"Okay, well just in case, extra utensils are in the drawer to your right. I'll be right back."

I went to the restroom to fluff up my hair, rinse my mouth out, and touch up my make-up. Since he went to all this trouble the least I could do was look presentable.

"Alice, I hope you're not in there fussing in the mirror. You already look beautiful to me," Carl yelled from the kitchen.

"I'll be right there."

I took a deep breath, fluffed my hair one more time, and returned.

"Everything smells wonderful. What did you decide to get?"

"We have your favorite Italian cuisine. Nothing but the best for the lady. As a matter of fact let me serve you. Have a seat."

"Carl, you don't have to..."

"Eh, eh. No arguing. Allow me to take care of you," he said.

He pulled out my chair for me.

"Tonight we have chicken piccata with lemon caper sauce. We also have a bottle of Chardonnay and a surprise dessert for your dining pleasure."

"Wow. You really put a lot of thought into everything, didn't you?"

"Yes, as I said. Only the best for you."

He poured a glass of wine for the two of us and then joined me at the table.

"Well, don't just sit there. Mangia, mangia!"

"Don't worry. You don't have to tell me twice."

We sat and ate quietly which was different for us. Normally we had so much to say. The food was delicious. Even the gesture was sweet. But something in the atmosphere was different with us tonight.

"Is everything okay with the food?"

"Oh yes, it couldn't be better."

"How about the wine?"

"It's perfect. Carl, you did a lovely job with dinner. There's absolutely nothing to complain about."

He smiled. "Well, it's not like I cooked it or anything. But, I tried my best."

"That, you did."

We continued to sit in awkward silence. The sound of the forks scraping along the plates became my point of focus. I knew I was consumed in my own thoughts after Stanley came over earlier, but I was afraid it was starting to show.

"Alice."

"Yes?"

"Is everything okay with you this evening? You don't seem like your usual bubbly self."

"I'm sorry, Carl. I guess I underestimated how tired I was."

"I hope you're not coming down with anything."

"No, I'll be fine. I'm sure it's nothing a good night's rest can't cure. I'm sorry for being such a party pooper."

"It's my fault. You tried to tell me earlier and I insisted on coming over just the same."

"Oh, Stanley... I mean... Carl. It's not your fault."

I took another bite into my food. There was no covering up the fact that I clearly called him Stanley out loud. What was I thinking? I was quietly screaming on the inside for being so stupid but on the outside I tried to gloss it over.

"Ahh, so maybe that's why you're so distracted this evening. Who's Stanley?"

I swallowed my last piece of chicken while praying for help to get out of this one.

"I don't know what I was thinking. Stanley is just a friend of mine. I really meant to say your name. That's how I know I'm tired. I'm getting all of my friends' names mixed up."

I tried not to ramble but I don't think it worked. Carl put his fork down and wiped his mouth with a napkin.

"Interesting," he said.

"What's interesting?"

"For the last few months I always thought you viewed me as more than just a friend. I guess I was wrong."

I'm certain this would normally be the time to respond with words of reassurance but I didn't know what to say.

"What makes you say a thing like that?"

"Well, for one thing, you just said 'I'm getting all my friends mixed up.' I figure that's a good indicator that you consider me to be one of your friends, don't you?"

"Stanley... Carl... ugh!" I dropped my fork down on the plate out of frustration. How could I be so careless to mess up his name twice? I was never one for putting on a good poker face. It was all going down hill from here.

"Carl. I apologize. I have a lot on my mind this evening and clearly I'm distracted."

"Stanley..." Carl was trying to jog his memory.

"He's the guy that saw us kissing on the front porch. I thought he was just a friend. Why would a friend have you so distracted?"

I took a deep breath.

"He is my friend. I haven't been involved with anyone romantically since you and I have been seeing one another. But... today he revealed his true feeling and..."

"Let me guess... you have feelings for him."

"I hadn't considered it until now. I always thought things were strictly platonic."

"But it's weighing on your mind, which means you are considering it now."

I quietly shook my head yes. I didn't have all the answers but I knew it was at least worth considering.

Carl started to gather his utensils and cleaned up his side of the table.

"Alice, that's disappointing for me to hear. I'd rather you tell me you're not interested at all. But, since you didn't, I think you need to take the time necessary to decide what you want to do. I'm not a selfish man, but I'd rather have your undivided attention."

He was right. Now that I reached this fork in the road, I needed to do something about it.

Carl stood and began clearing our plates.

"I'll get the dishes. Please don't worry about that." I reached over to take the plates. He reached back and held my hand.

"Whatever you decide just know that I genuinely do care about you."

I put the plates down and gave Carl a hug. He could've handled this evening so many different ways but chose to take the high road, and for that I was grateful.

He began to gather his things to leave.

"Are you leaving without having dessert?" I asked.

"Yeah, I think you need time to be alone, like you were graciously requesting earlier. I feel terrible for not listening to you."

"Oh, Carl, don't be foolish. You can stay and eat dessert."

"No. Trust me. It's the perfect comfort food for times like this. The restaurant included plastic forks in the bag. Kick up your feet, put on a good movie, and eat until your heart is content."

"Are you sure?"

"I'm sure."

He kissed my hand, wished me a good night, and left.

After locking the door I returned to the kitchen to see what he brought for dessert. He was right. Cheesecake was the perfect comfort food. Now that I think about it... two men had walked in and out of my door today. However, the only thing providing me with any real comfort tonight was my couch and a piece of cheesecake.

PAYTON

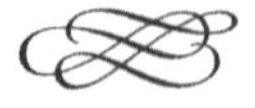

The months that followed flew by so quickly I could barely keep up. Cole finally got his cast off but walked with a little limp. And, at the store, Abby was helping out since Natalie needed to take time to be with her mother who was ill.

"How's everything going with wedding planning?"

"If you would've asked me this question even a week ago I would've responded differently. But, now that the DJ has been secured I can't think of anything else to plan."

"Really? Go girl! With two months left what on earth are you going to do with yourself?"

"Ha ha!"

"I'm being serious. I thought you would be planning all the way up until the last hour."

"I thought so, too. I went over my checklist multiple times. Hair, make-up, food, the cake, the photographer, the rental company, the invitations, and rsvp's. Cole even has his suit picked out. And, with you, Rebecca, and Emmie wearing different shades of mauve, I don't see how we can go wrong."

"Oh, okay. What about your honeymoon?"

"All set. We're going to Tahiti. I'm so excited about it. I can't remember the last time I took a real vacation."

"Um, last time I checked you're getting married on the beach and will be living in a beach house when you return from your honeymoon. Your whole life is centered around one big vacation. Now what about Emmie? Is she staying with Alice while you're in Tahiti?"

"Yes, Alice is such a Godsend. I can't think of one time she hasn't made herself available to look after Emmie when needed."

"I wonder if she's going to feel lonely once you move in. Think about it. You will be there, so there won't be a need for her to worry about taking care of Emmie. I mean, I'm sure you guys will still welcome her to come around whenever she wants to visit, but still."

"Honestly, I think she'll be fine. She may miss some of the routines, but the last time we had a chance to chat it seemed like her love life was keeping her on her toes."

"Oh?" Abby seemed intrigued.

"Yeah. We should have another get-together with just the ladies. That way we can invite Alice and play catch up."

"What about Rebecca? I think she's just starting to get into some sort of groove with John William. I doubt she'll want to break the routine."

"It doesn't have to be an overnight event or anything major. We'll work out something that's conducive to everyone's schedule."

"Sounds good to me."

I climbed the step ladder to grab a few items on the top shelf. The bells on the front door rang. There was something about hearing the sound of those bells that reminded me of an old fashioned store.

"What are you doing here?" I overheard Abby say.

"I'm here to see Payton." The male voice sounded all too familiar. It was my ex-husband, Jack. I froze on the step stool.

"Jack, the last time you showed up uninvited, Payton asked you never to come around again. I remember it clearly because I was at my parents' house that day."

"I need to talk to Payton."

"What you need to do is leave before I call the cops."

"Payton?" I could hear Jack calling my name but I didn't want to respond. It felt like I was in the midst of a bad dream and all the life was being drained right out of me.

"Jack, are you listening to me? I said leave!"

"I got it, Abby," I said. She gave me a disappointed look. I couldn't blame her. I was disappointed in me, too, but I decided to let him speak to me anyway.

"Jack, what are you doing here?"

"I need to talk to you for a minute. Can we speak in private?"

I stepped down and looked around the store while debating whether this was a good idea.

"We won't be long, Abby."

He followed me to the back room.

"Yell if you need me." Abby threw a few daggers his way before returning to the front counter.

In the back I leaned against my work table and waited for him to speak. He was sweating and reeked of alcohol.

He stepped closer.

"Back up."

"You know I wouldn't harm you, Payton."

"That's not the point. I'm more comfortable with you staying back."

He put his hands up and backed away.

"I'll stand over here."

We stood in silence for a while.

"What do you want?"

"You."

I proceeded to start walking out of the room.

"Please. Payton, please don't go. I came all this way to talk to you please."

"The distance you traveled is your own fault. I told you the last time to leave me and my family alone."

He glanced down at my hand.

"Is that an engagement ring on your finger?"

I looked away while twirling the ring with my finger. This whole situation was uncomfortable and making me nervous.

"The ring is irrelevant, Jack. I'm going to ask you one last time. What do you want?"

The pitiful look on his face as he stood there sniffling made me angry and sad at the same time.

"I want you to take me back. It's been too long, Payton. I need you. Take me back."

He stumbled forward a few steps and started crying.

"Are you drunk?"

"I'm lonely. I miss you. Nobody has ever loved me the way you did, Payton. Nobody."

"So let me get this right. You're drunk and nobody has ever loved you the way that I did. That's interesting. So basically you had to run through a lot of women first to figure this out. Got it. Is there anything else you want to tell me?"

"That's not how it happened."

"Newsflash. I don't care to know how it happened. I'm an engaged woman now, Jack. Now that you're here, I get to thank you personally for freeing me up so that I could meet the love of my life."

"I can't believe you're getting married. How could you, Payton?"

"What! How could I? I can't believe you would even fix your face to ask me something like that. Oh, I'm sorry. I guess I was supposed to just sit around and wait for you to finish getting acquainted with every woman in the state of Connecticut? Let's not forget that you divorced me, by the way. I guess you forgot that part."

"I didn't forget. I was stupid, I know."

"You are stupid to think I would wait until you figured out how to keep your pants zipped up."

He slid down the wall and sat covering his face. His cry sounded pathetic. I almost felt sorry for him.

"Do you love him?" he asked.

"I wouldn't be marrying him if I didn't. But this isn't about me, Jack. It's not even about us anymore. It hasn't been for a long time. You need help. You've been looking for love in all the wrong places, and now that you've finally hit rock bottom, you need help!"

Abby walked in quietly but Jack didn't even notice with his head hanging and all the crying. She mouthed the word 'Wow' to me and then turned around and left.

"I guess you're right. I keep looking for someone or something to soothe my pain. But it's not working. None of it is working. The job is threatening to put me on probation, the bank accounts are almost tapped out. I feel like I don't have anything left to live for. It's like I've lost my sense of purpose. That's why I came here to talk to you. The last time I remember having a stable life and feeling loved was when I was with you."

I passed him a box of tissues. There was nothing more pitiful than seeing a man who had finally hit rock bottom. Even though I was angry at him I still had a heart.

"As much as you hurt me I don't wish this on my worse enemy."

While remaining as distant as I possibly could I joined him on the floor.

"It's totally fair if you viewed me as your worst enemy. I deserve it," he said.

"That's part of the problem."

"What?"

"You're still wallowing around in your own mess. It's time to pick your head up and start living your new life. That's what I had to learn to do."

"What if I don't want a new life? What if I just want to return to what was good?"

"I didn't want to start a new life either. I was thrusted into it. We don't always get what we want, Jack. And, I'm grateful for it. Turns out that not everything we want is what's best for us anyway."

"So, what's his name?" he asked.

"No. We're not doing this. I'm not getting into the details of my life. What good would it do you to know anyway?"

He laughed while blowing his nose.

"You were always the more mature one of the two of us. I guess some things never change."

"I guess." I rolled my eyes.

"Hey, Jack?"

"Yes."

"What are you doing here in Florida and how in the world did you find my store?"

"I'm here on business and heading back to Connecticut tomorrow. I found the store by googling your name."

"Mmm."

"Payton, it may not mean much to you, but I'm really sorry for hurting you and breaking up our marriage. You were the perfect wife back then and I know you will be going forward."

"Thank you, Jack. But what about you? The idea that your

life is over couldn't be further from the truth. I don't care what you have to do. Find a therapist to talk to if you need someone to lean on. Whatever you do, don't lose your job and keep chasing after things that leave you feeling empty inside."

I don't know how I was able to find it in my heart to actually care. But I did. After all that Jack had done to me, I didn't have a mean bone in my body, and didn't wish him any harm. I guess that's what happens when you finally start to heal from your brokenness.

"I created quite a mess for myself back home. All the drinking, and gambling, and the women. It felt like one day I woke up in a complete fog, not knowing where I was or how I had gotten there."

"I'm surprised things spiraled so far out of control. You weren't like this when we first met. What happened?"

"If I'm honest, by the time we were engaged the signs were already there. I just did a good job at hiding it from you and your family."

"Hiding what?"

"Let's just say I made a lot of dumb choices to climb my way up the corporate ladder and fit in with the old boy's club. I went to all the parties, started tossing around money I didn't have to look impressive, gambled, drank."

He held his head down in shame.

"And, even slept around just to prove that I was one of them."

I closed my eyes but I wasn't shocked. If anything he was confirming a lot of my suspicions.

"Did it work?"

"What do you mean did it work?"

"Did you get what you wanted?"

"Initially. But in the long run, no. What do I have to show for it? No wife, no assets, and I'm about to lose my job if I don't get my act together. To make matters worse, my two best friends Whiskey and Rum are all I have to lean on. How's that for getting what I wanted?"

"Wow."

It looked like I had dodged a huge bullet.

"You know, Jack. For a moment you almost had me feeling sorry for you. But, the more I sit here and think about it, you're still just as selfish as ever."

"Gee, thanks. Kick me when I'm already feeling low."

"You have to quit with all the whoa is me nonsense. You came here for yourself, not for me. You're chasing after something or someone that will make you feel better, help you keep your job, or return back to a so called normal life. And, you woke up this morning with this bright idea that finding me was the solution. But you're wrong. I can't do anything to help you even if I wanted to, Jack. You have to want to make better choices for yourself. When I asked you 'did it work?' Your response to me was 'initially, but in the long run, no.' That's the problem... that's your enemy right there. You actually believe that it worked at some point. The lifestyle you chose never worked. You were just deceiving yourself. Even when it felt good and seemed glamorous, you were still a train wreck waiting to happen."

Jack leaned back against the wall.

"I'm no expert, but I can only imagine how much better off you'd be if you stop being so self-centered. You're always trying to get something rather than give."

"You're probably right."

I stood up and dusted my pants off. He reached out his hand for me to assist him with getting up.

"I'm ten times lighter than you, Jack Saunders. Here, grab on to this chair."

"Ha, you always were a tiny little thing."

While standing upright he looked into my eyes.

"Tiny, blond, and as beautiful as the day I met you. Some things never change."

"Don't do that."

"Don't do what? Pay you a compliment? Tell you the truth? Show you that I was a fool for letting you go? I'd be a fool not to try, Payton."

"You're a part of my past, Jack... a piece of history that I no longer want to relive. Part of me wants to give you a piece of my mind and tell you right where you can go."

"Like you did that time I showed up at your parents' house?"

"Exactly."

"Please don't. Hear me out this time. I know I'm a mess right now, but hear my heart. It's crying out to you, Payton. It has been for a long time now."

I turned away and looked at the cork board filled with tasks for the week.

"I don't wish you any ill will but ..."

Cole's voice echoed abruptly from the other side of the room.

"It's time for you to leave," he said.

I turned around to see Cole standing at the door with Abby a few feet behind him. Her eyes were wide open watching every bit of the scene as it unfolded. I felt nauseous.

"Don't you think that's up to Payton to decide?" Jack said.

"It's my understanding she made her decision clear to you a long time ago. Your visit today is unwelcome."

Everyone looked at me.

"You can't keep doing this, Jack. I moved on and now it's time that you do the same."

"Payton, you were softening up to me before he walked into the room. Admit it. You know you were."

Before I could answer good, Cole walked over to Jack with his slight limp.

"I'm giving you one last chance to leave out of here with some dignity. If you don't, I will personally remove you out of here myself."

Jack glanced over at me.

"Leave, Jack."

He brushed past Cole and Abby and stormed his way out of the room. As soon as he left, every emotion and all the tears that I didn't know I had left resurfaced. Cole came closer to console me.

"Are you alright?"

"I'm fine."

I wiped away the tears as quickly as possible.

"I'm sorry. I don't know why I'm crying."

He held me close.

"You two were married. I would imagine it's normal to still have a sore spot. When somebody hurts you the way he did that kind of healing doesn't take place overnight."

My temples were throbbing but it felt good to close my eyes and rest on his shoulders.

"Are you having any doubts or second thoughts?"

"About what?"

"Us."

"Oh, God, no. I'm very certain about us. He came by here unannounced. He said he was here on business. Please don't ever doubt my feelings for you for one second. I love you, Cole."

"I love you, too. I don't doubt that you love me. It's just that he mentioned something about you softening up to him, so I didn't know."

"I admit that I felt sorry for him, but not so sorry that I would ever want him back. He has drinking problems, money problems, and even problems at work. It just blows my mind how much he's changed, that's all.

"You deserve better, my love. You deserve much, much better. I plan to spend the rest of my life giving you all that you deserve and more."

Abby knocked at the entrance of the break room to let us know she was still standing there.

"Okay you two. Break up the love fest for now. Would somebody mind filling me in on what happened?"

Cole and I looked at each other and laughed.

"It's not funny. One minute sloppy Jack shows up and wants to talk, then I come to check on you, Payton, and he's on the floor crying, then next thing I know here comes Cole to the rescue."

Now that Abby mentioned it I wondered what brought Cole into the store during the middle of the morning.

"Why did you stop by, babe?"

"What's the matter? You don't like when I surprise you anymore?" He teased.

"No, that's not it. I was just wondering if there was anything in particular that you needed."

"Honestly, I just came back from giving an estimate and wanted to stop in and say hello. I had no idea what I was walking in to."

"Well, your timing couldn't be more perfect, Cole. I was hoping you would give him a knuckle sandwich, just to show him who's boss." Abby held both fists in the air like a boxer.

"Ha! I'll have to keep that in mind for next time."

"Next time? Hopefully there won't be a next time," I said.

"If it were me I wouldn't sit around hoping. I'd get a restraining order just to let him know that I mean business. I know you're too nice for that Payton, but it's just a thought."

"Abby, a restraining order? Really? It's just Jack. He's hasn't been around in all this time."

"I know! And then poof, out of nowhere he shows up. What if you were here by yourself? Maybe you should get yourself a weapon to hide in here just in case."

"That's not a bad idea, Payton." Cole agreed.

"Look you guys. I already have a headache. Let's get back out front and talk about all this later."

The remainder of the day I was distracted with images of Jack crying on the floor and begging me to take him back. I had to repeatedly remind myself that what he was going through wasn't my fault. My best days laid ahead in my future with Cole and that's where my focus belonged.

PAYTON

I loved it when the ladies got together to play catch up. It had been so long since we kept up with any of our regular gatherings. Perhaps that was life's way of showing us that things were changing. However, if only for a few hours, we were looking forward to being together.

"Listen to that beautiful sound. I could literally fall asleep out here." I helped set up the canopy before stretching out on my beach chair.

The waves gently crashed on the shore. Without a cloud in sight and nothing but the sound of the ocean water it was absolutely heavenly.

"You take after your father, Payton. When we first retired I used to wonder how he quickly managed to fall into a daily nap routine. But now I'm convinced it's the sound of the ocean that mesmerizes him every time," mom said as she lathered sunscreen all over her legs.

"Helen, how is Will doing? I haven't seen him in a while," Alice asked.

"He's okay. Sadly, he spends most of his days inside. It's

almost as if the dementia has caused him to retreat from the outside world. He's comfortable within the confines of his home and doesn't really socialize as much. That part breaks my heart."

"Mom, I've been thinking about dad's health as it pertains to the wedding. Do you think he'll still be comfortable with walking me down the aisle?"

"Your father wouldn't have it any other way, Payton."

Rebecca and Abby approached the canopy dragging a large cooler from the house.

"Dad wouldn't have what any other way?" Rebecca asked.

"We were talking about whether or not he would be feeling up to walking Payton down the aisle."

"Oh, I don't see why not. Dad walked me down the aisle just a few months ago. Even though our ceremony was on a much smaller scale. Much... much... smaller."

"Gosh, don't downplay it, Rebecca. It was still a beautiful celebration of your union with Ethan. And, how special was it to have all of your immediate family members there?" Abby said.

"It just felt like we had to hurry up and get hitched before I gave birth. Don't get me wrong. I loved how everyone showed their support. The celebration at the restaurant afterward was very sweet. But let's be real. If I wasn't pregnant at the time, you know I would've done things totally different."

"Okay, so when you're ready the two of you can have a do over of some sort. Go all out and invite the whole town."

"We were actually talking about it recently."

I laughed. Leave it to Rebecca to already be planning her second wedding.

Mom leaned over and spoke to Alice in a loud enough voice where we could all still hear.

"Alice, are you sure you want to join forces with the Matthews? We can be kind of crazy, you know."

Alice chuckled.

"You don't know crazy until you've had a chance to hang out with me. With all the drama I've been through lately, forget it. As for you all, I can't think of any other family I'd rather join forces with. I certainly couldn't ask for a better daughter-in-law than Payton."

"Aww, Alice, that's so sweet." I blew Alice a kiss.

"You know I love you, dear. We all do."

"I love you, too. But, is everything okay with you? This is the first time I'm hearing you mention drama."

"Everything will be fine. Just working out a few kinks in my life, that's all."

"Wait, is this about the two guys you were telling us about?"

Alice nodded her head.

"Two men? Whoo hooo, go Alice! Must be nice to have options." Rebecca pretended like she was waving a lasso around.

"Rebecca, will you hush. It's not like that," I said.

"Actually, that's exactly what it's like. Both Stanley and Carl have expressed an interest in pursuing a relationship. I have to decide which one I want to be with. Or decide to remain alone. Either way there's a decision to be made."

Alice had our full attention.

"Okay, clearly I'm out of the loop. What did I miss?" Abby lowered her sunglasses.

"Yeah, that makes two of us. Who's Stanley and Carl?" Rebecca added.

"You haven't missed much. When we went shopping for a wedding dress with Payton I filled them in on my not so interesting love life. The short version is that my long time friend,

Stanley found out that I was seeing someone. This upset him because he had hopes of us being together. I didn't know how he felt because he's more of the quiet type. His actions speak louder than words is the way he described it. The sad part is I've always received his actions as friendly gestures. I just thought he was being nice. Carl on the other hand is..."

"Romantic, he makes her feel alive, and he causes her to blush when she talks about him." Mom filled in the blanks.

"Well, if that's the case, then you have your answer. Case closed," Rebecca said.

"I wish it was that simple."

"Why isn't it?"

"I've been asking myself the same question for the last several weeks. I told them both I needed a little time and haven't really addressed it since. Carl is really good about doing all the things that make me feel like a teenager in love. He brings me roses and plans romantic evenings for two. But you and I both know that doesn't last forever. My level of distraction started becoming really obvious on our last date. He brought over a nice meal but I couldn't even stay focused long enough to enjoy it. All I remember thinking about is how Stanley has always been there for me as a friend, how he takes care of my needs without me even asking, and how he pays attention to all of my favorite things."

"You mean like the Chamomile tea and pound cake?" I asked.

"That's exactly what I mean. How could I possibly choose Carl and overlook the one who's been there for me all along?"

"Alice, it's not your fault. Stanley could've said something long before Carl showed up."

"You know, Payton, I thought the same thing at first. But as he mentioned, that's just not his way. Have you ever met the kind of man that may not be the most expressive or affectionate but you know they care for you by the little things they do? Stanley fixes things that I don't even know are broken. He routinely brings my favorite treats every Thursday..."

"I don't know, Alice. Routines can get old very quickly." Mom grumbled as if it was personal.

"Helen, you've been married longer than any of us. Wouldn't you rather live life with your best friend rather than someone who gives you a passing thrill?"

"I guess you're right, Alice. Will has always been my best friend."

"Well, it sounds like this love triangle has officially come to an end. All you have to do is kick Carl to the curb and pass Stanley the toolbox. There, problem solved. Next?" Rebecca kicked her feet up and pulled her sun hat forward.

"You make it sound so easy. I should've consulted with you weeks ago." Alice teased.

"Alice, if you don't mind me asking, if this happened weeks ago, why haven't you mentioned your feelings to Stanley?" Abby asked as she sat up to apply more sunscreen.

"This seems a little silly but I don't know why. A part of me is worried that I ruined everything after he saw me kissing Carl on the front porch. Even though he did come to see me at the house afterward. Then there's the other concern... what if we pursue something more but find out we were better off as friends?"

"Whoa whoa whoa.... hold your horses. No one mentioned a word about any kissing." Rebecca began to make a scene but Mom shut her down really quick.

"Rebecca!" she scolded.

Abby thought it was hysterical and so did Alice.

"Mom, why are you so surprised? You know Rebecca doesn't have a filter."

"Okay, in my defense, I must've missed that part of the

story. Alice, I apologize but I'm notorious for being the outspoken one in the family. If most are thinking it, I'll say it!"

Rebecca wasn't lying but thankfully Alice didn't seem to care.

"There's no need to apologize, dear. I love your candor. And, to answer your question, we did exchange our first kiss. However, I'd take it all back if I could. Look at all the hurt it's caused."

"Alice, I don't have nearly as much experience with love as you and mom. But, if I could offer my two cents..." I felt like the writing was on the wall but didn't want to overstep my boundaries.

"Please do."

"Go talk to Stanley. He sounds like a diamond in the rough and it's obvious that you care for him. I'd much rather see you with your best friend than caught up in a magical fairy tale that will quickly fade away."

"You know, Payton, I think you're right. Perhaps this Thursday I can pay him a visit and bring him his favorite meal as a peace offering. At least it's a start."

"Whoo hoo, that's what I'm talking about. Bring your man a home cooked meal!" With all the hooting you would've thought Rebecca was at a baseball game.

"Rebecca, I think you need to get out more," I said.

"Honestly, I'm so excited to have a little free time I don't know what to do with myself. I love Ethan and John William, but if I didn't get out of the house soon, I was about to lose my mind."

"Well, why didn't you say something? You know I'd be happy to spend more time with my grandson if you need a break." Mom always thought the more the merrier when it came to having the grandkids around.

"You already watch him once a week. I didn't want to be overbearing."

"There's no such thing when it comes to my grandkids. Anytime you need a break just let me know. I need a change in pace every once in a while."

"I bet we all could benefit from a change in pace. Maybe next year we should plan a family vacation," I suggested.

"That's not a bad idea," mom said.

Abby pulled a soda out of the cooler. "Yeah, I can just see it now. All of the moms will need another vacation just from trying to keep up with all the kids... and the husbands for that matter!"

We continued to lay under the canopy and have girl talk for as long as our schedules would allow. After grabbing lunch, everyone left to tend to their afternoon plans.

~

I decided to spend a quiet Sunday afternoon at the store catching up on paperwork.

The first item on my agenda was to go through all of my voicemails. I pulled out a sketchpad to take notes.

'Hi Payton, this is Cindy from Cindy's Florals. I have a suggestion to make regarding your order for the wedding. Just a couple of adjustments that will help to enhance your table arrangements. When you get a chance give me a call. Thanks.'

I skipped on to the next message.

'Payton, hi. This is Natalie. I tried to reach you on your cell but thought I should call the store as well. When you get a chance please call me back. Talk to you soon."

I hope she had good news. I was starting to fall behind on a few things and really needed her help at the store.

I pressed the button to play the final message but was interrupted by the bells ringing on the front door.

"I'm sorry, we're closed on Sundays."

I turned around and started to explain further but froze in my tracks at the sight before me.

"Payton, it's me, Jack."

"What are you doing here? I thought we asked you to leave."

He took a step toward me but I backed away.

"Please, Payton, I hate it when you back away from me like that. You don't have to be afraid. I just came back so we could talk alone."

"How did you know I'd be here? The store is normally closed on Sundays."

"I didn't know. I extended my trip a few days and decided to drive by and take a chance to see if you were here. That's all. Honest to God, Payton. I'm here with good intentions. Look at me. I cleaned myself up. I haven't had anything to drink within the last couple of days. I'm taking your advice and working on getting myself together. It's not going to happen overnight but I started, and that's what matters most, right?"

"Yeah, I guess. I just don't understand why you felt the need to come back here. You're putting me in a very awkward position. I'm an engaged woman, Jack. You can't just show up whenever you want and expect me to be here for you."

Jack wasn't intimidating but he did catch me by surprise. He was cleaned up with a fresh out of the shower smell and dressed nice in his golf clothes... similar to the way he looked when we first met.

"I promise to walk right back out the door if you want me to. All you have to do is say the word, Payton. I only came back because I could hear the sound of hesitation in your voice when we spoke yesterday. You would've talked with me further if we hadn't been interrupted. We haven't been apart so long that I can't recognize that sound in my wife's voice. Tell me I'm wrong and I'll leave."

"I'm not your wife anymore, Jack."

"You may not be but the love is still there and the bond is still there. You can't just turn it off like a switch."

"You did."

"I admit I was wrong. Dead wrong for how I treated you. I'll admit it a thousand times if you want me to, but there's no denying that we still have a connection, Payton. I felt it when we were talking. Yesterday you did something that no one has done in a long time. You listened to me. You heard what I had to say. Yeah, you were mad at me but you cared. You can't deny that you still care, Payton. I can see it in your eyes."

I relaxed my body against the counter feeling rather defeated because Jack was right.

"I guess you got me."

"What?"

"You figured me out. You're calling my bluff. I do care but that doesn't mean that I think we should be together."

He took a few steps closer and lowered his voice to a soft whisper. I could feel my heart racing.

"Payton, underneath that protective shell that you created against me is a woman who still loves me. I can feel it."

Jack's lips softly touched mine. I was lost in a momentary state of shock, but not for long before I hauled off and smacked him across his face.

"Jack... you have approximately sixty seconds to get out of my store."

He held his hand up to his cheek.

"Payton."

"Fifty-nine."

"Payton, please."

"Fifty-eight."

He took a few steps backward and proceeded to leave.

"Jack, one more thing before you go. If you ever set foot around me again you will be arrested."

"I didn't hurt you."

"It doesn't matter. You'll be in violation of the restraining order that I'm about to file. Consider this to be your last warning."

As soon as he left I ran to lock the door. I watched him get in his car across the street and glance back at me before closing the door. Every encounter with Jack felt like one tumultuous experience after the other. This time I hoped would be the last.

ALICE

"Stanley, can we talk?"

He slowly backed away from the threshold of the front door to let me in. Stanley usually didn't say much unless he was speaking about his military days or making his case for why something needed to be fixed.

"Come on in."

"I brought your favorite roasted chicken with a side of mashed potatoes and gravy. I made sure to include the baby carrots that you like."

"Thank you. You didn't have to do that."

"I wanted to."

He moved a few papers off the kitchen counter to make room for the food.

"Here, uh, I guess we can set the plate over here. If I would've known you were coming I could've made arrangements for you to have your usual. I just assumed you weren't interested."

"Oh, don't worry about it, Stanley. I know your heart."

"Do you?"

I paused in awkward silence.

"I would say so. I know your heart now better than I ever have before."

He placed his hands in his pockets and started making his way back to the living room.

"Stanley, that's actually why I came over today. I'd like to pick up where we left off in conversation if it's alright with you."

He took a seat in his corner rocking chair and folded his hands.

"I suppose there's no harm in talking. Of course, you already know how I feel."

"Yes, about that. A lot has changed since we last spoke. I guess I should start by saying that I'm no longer seeing Carl."

I waited to see if I would get a rise out of Stanley, but he remained silent.

"Stanley, I don't know where to begin. What can I say?"

"Just say what's on your mind. I can handle it."

"Okay."

I took a deep breath.

"When you and I first met I viewed you as someone who would be nice to get to know. I figured we'd take our time and enjoy one another's company, and see where it would lead."

"Mm hmm," he responded.

"Then we fell into a routine of coming over once or twice a week... and... I didn't know what to make of it. The gestures of bringing tea and fixing things were sweet, but for me, it didn't automatically equate to a relationship. So I just assumed that we were good friends who liked to keep each other company."

"Mm hmm."

"I guess I missed the cues. However, there's one thing that's become obvious to me during this time. You and I do have a special bond. You take good care of me and I know I can call on you for anything. Plus, I can't think of anyone else that I'd rather spend my tea time with but you."

"You mean you still want me to come around?"

"That's exactly what I mean."

"And you're sure I won't catch old lover boy trying to kiss you on the front porch again?"

"Haha! That's an interesting way to put it. No, you won't see him anymore and neither will I."

"I never could figure out what you saw in that guy in the first place. Who goes around wearing a sweater vest over your shirt in hot sunny Florida for goodness sake."

It was nice to be able to break the ice and feel comfortable with each other again.

"All jokes aside, I have to take ownership of my part. My late wife used to get on my case for the same things that you mentioned. She used to say 'Stan, it wouldn't hurt for you to be a little romantic every once in a while.' It's not that I didn't care to. Daddy and Papaw just weren't overly affectionate men and I guess the trait wound up in my genes, whether I asked for it or not. But I'll tell you one lesson I've learned. I'm not about to let another wonderful lady pass me by without changing my ways."

He came over to join me on the couch and took me by the hand.

"When I didn't hear from you I thought I lost you, Alice. I guess technically you were never mine to begin with, but I'd like to change that. I promise to come out of my shell more if that will make you happy."

"Oh, Stanley, that's so sweet. Look at you. Your cheeks are turning red."

"Hey, I'm as rusty as they come at this whole romance thing but I'll tell you this. I know a good woman when I see one. You, Alice Miller, are a good woman, and I enjoy being with you and making you happy."

"You, Stanley Baker, are a good man."

"I try to be. You know a lot of things about me, Alice. But there's one thing I've never shared with anyone that I think you should know."

"What is it?"

He hesitated.

"Many marriages go through hard times. Some harder than others as I'm sure you probably experienced when you were married."

"Of course."

"Anne and me went through something that most probably would've gotten a divorce over. Around our twentieth wedding anniversary, we had been through one of the toughest times imaginable. I was retired from the Army by then and spent most of my days still taking on some government contract work. Anne stayed at home and... I guess you could say we had grown distant for a period of time. The kids were no longer kids and had their own lives, and I think all of it combined left Anne feeling rather lonely. A long time friend of ours used to check in and come to her aid at times when I couldn't be there. He bailed us out of tight situations so many times. One time the car broke down. Another time a pipe burst and you name it, he was there. But, I'll never forget the day I came home early to find him and Anne together. No man ever wants to see the woman he loves with someone else."

I had a flashback to the moment with Carl on the porch. When I looked up Stanley looked so broken hearted. I felt awful.

"Stanley, I'm so sorry."

"Alice, that was a long time ago. And, I'm not telling you this story for your sympathy. You didn't do anything to be sorry about. Although it was a rough road ahead for a while to come, I eventually went on to forgive Anne. I knew deep down she had a good heart and that wasn't to be confused with what she had done. Like I said, it took a while for me to come to that conclusion but I did. That should hopefully give you some insight into the kind of man I am. I may not win first prize for knowing how to sweep a woman off her feet but I'm loyal, I'm here for you when you need me. Hopefully, that's what matters most to you."

"It matters more than you know. I wish I could turn back the clock and take away that moment that you witnessed me kissing someone else. I'm surprised you want to have anything to do with me given what you've shared."

"Nooo, Alice."

Stanley grabbed me by the hand.

"I don't see it that way at all. I didn't speak up and tell you how I felt about you and we weren't an item. There's a big difference."

He inched closer and gave me a peck on the lips. Feeling his lips for the first time ignited a spark. It's funny how love works. Perhaps Stanley was all the spice I really needed and just didn't see it right away.

He drew me in even closer. I had to remind myself to breathe.

"I've been wanting to kiss you for a long time. But, I'll take it easy... don't want to get too far ahead of myself and scare you off." He chuckled.

"I don't think you would know how to scare me off, Stanley."

"Well, that's good to know."

"What do you say we heat up your food so you can enjoy a nice hot meal?" I offered.

"You won't get any arguments out of me."

I happily followed him into the kitchen. My heart was full and I was at peace again knowing I had made the right decision.

PAYTON

We arrived at the bakery for the cake tasting with time to spare. The owner was kind to set up a table with a window view and gave us a catalog of options to look through as we waited for the appointment to begin.

"Wow, there are so many designs and so many options I wouldn't know where to begin," Cole said as he closed the catalog.

"Giving up so soon? We're just getting started."

"Babe, the design, the amount of tiers, that's all up to you. If you really want my input I'll give it to you but I'm all about the taste. I vote for anything that tastes good. I'll take chocolate, red velvet, vanilla, you name it."

"You're easy to please."

"Yep, I like to keep things nice and simple."

I felt heavily distracted with thoughts of Jack's visit swimming around in my head but I tried to stay focused. I could vaguely hear Cole tapping his fingers to the tune of the music in the background. I continued to listen to the sound as I watched a red fire truck drive down the street.

"Payton... Payton!"

"Huh?"

"Are you alright? You don't seem like yourself today."

"I'm fine. Why, what's the matter?"

"Nothing, I was starting to tell you they finally got back to me about the cause of the house fire."

"The house fire?"

"Yeah, remember the fire that caused me to break my leg?"

"Yes, yes, of course. What did they say?"

"It was my client's son and his friends. They were cooking something and left it unattended on the stove. He says he completely forgot about it."

"Wow, what a costly mistake."

"Tell me about it. They're still not back in the house. It will probably be a while before they get to move back in again."

"Forget the house. That fire could've cost you your life." I snapped.

"I know... but it didn't."

"I at least hope they were apologetic."

We were interrupted by Ms. Taylor, the owner of the bakery.

"May I interest you in some fine cake options for your wedding?"

The aroma from the cake samples were to die for. Every piece looked mouth watering and inviting.

"I'm going to position the tray just so. Before we begin I'd love to give you a little introduction if you will."

"Sure," I said.

"Taylor's Bakery is new to the Pelican Beach area but not new to the cake industry. We've been baking and designing wedding cakes among others for well over thirty-five years. The recipes began with my great-grandmother and were passed down from generation to generation. Today, I will be presenting to you some of our most popular options. However, if you decide that you want us to create a custom combination of flavors we can do that for you as well. Shall we begin?"

"Yes, ma'am." Cole held his fork in ready position.

"First up, we have our famous chocolate champagne cake. There's no doubt that this choice will wake your taste buds up."

He was the first to dig in.

"Yess, this is amazing."

Ms. Taylor checked in with me.

"It's good, but maybe a little too rich for the occasion."

"Okay, how about our next choice which is red velvet with a delicious cream cheese frosting."

This time Cole fed me a piece of cake.

"Practicing for the reception?"

"Absolutely. What do you think?" he said.

"Umm, again, it's good. It just reminds me of a birthday cake. What do you think?"

"It's another winner if you ask me. Hey, like I said, this is really on you, Payton. So far, I love them all."

"Ms. Taylor..."

"Please, call me Betty."

"Betty, what about a marble cake? Or a plain cake with a little raspberry filling? I'm looking for something that will hopefully please everyone. Something a little bit more balanced."

"Well, unfortunately, I don't know that you'll be able to please everyone but we certainly can suggest some of the more traditional flavors if you'd like."

"Yes, traditional works. Let's try some more traditional options."

"I don't know, Pay. Shouldn't this cake be about what 'we' like?"

"Of course we're going to pick a cake we like... I just think we should consider our guests as well."

Perhaps Cole wanted to have more of a say so than he originally thought. Either way, we continued to taste several cakes until my pallet was confused. Plus, I was full. Ms. Taylor suggested that making another appointment might be helpful so that we could return for a fresh start.

~

During the car ride home Cole continued to question if something was wrong.

"Payton, you're not acting like yourself. Now, you can keep pretending but I'd much rather you just come out with it and tell me what's bothering you. Maybe I can help."

"There's nothing you can do. The problem has already been resolved. I've just been trying to find the right time to tell you."

"Pay, what is it? You know you can tell me anything."

"Jack came by the store again last night."

"Okay... did you call the police?"

"No. Last night after he left I gathered all my things and went back to my parents' house to finish my work."

"Is that the reason why you sent me a text instead of calling me back last night?"

"I just needed time to think, Cole. I needed to get a game plan together to ensure this doesn't happen again."

"I don't understand why you wouldn't involve me. My job is to help protect you as best as I can. You and Emmie mean the world to me. What would you have done if he showed up at our house? Would you keep that to yourself, too?"

My eyes started to well up with tears. I hadn't considered what I would do in that situation, but I also didn't think Jack was a physical threat. He was more of a threat to my emotions than anything else.

"Talk to me, Payton. I feel like there's something you're not telling me."

"I don't think he would harm a fly, Cole."

"Then why isn't he respecting your boundaries?"

"I don't know. I think he's going through it right now."

"What exactly did he say to you?"

I knew Cole would be disappointed but it was best I tell him everything for the sake of our future marriage.

"He came back to tell me that he wanted to be with me. I guess he called himself catching me at a time when no one else would be around. He told me he was having problems financially, at his job, and he basically admitted that he was wrong for what he did."

"You're darn right he was wrong. He's also wrong for coming around you like this. Doesn't he know you're engaged?"

"He knows... but he tried to convince me to take him back... and..."

"And what?"

"He kissed me."

Cole stopped at a traffic light and continued to stare straight ahead.

"Should I be worried?"

"Cole, no. Not for one second. You are the only one for me. Jack is the one having a hard time understanding that, not me."

"I swear if I was there I would've punched him square in the face."

"Oh, I think I smacked him hard enough for the both of us."

"You did?"

"Yep. He had it coming. Look, I'm not going to sit here and pretend that he wasn't someone that I cared for deeply. Even though he did me wrong I hate to see him or anyone else hit rock bottom. But, I want to be very clear about where I stand.

You, Cole Miller, are my present and my future. It's you, Emmie, and me until the end."

He reached his hand across the center console and placed it on mine.

"Thank you, Pay. I know you didn't ask for this. It's an awful position to be in. I just look forward to a time when he's truly a thing of the past. In the meantime, what are we going to do to ensure this doesn't happen again?"

"I don't know that there's anything we can do. I told him I was going to file a restraining order but I don't know if it would fly since Jack isn't a physical threat."

"I beg to differ. A kiss is physical. Way too physical if you ask me."

I gave Cole a side eye knowing that he was being facetious.

"You know what I mean."

"Did he mention when he was catching his flight back to Connecticut?"

"I think he left today if I'm not mistaken."

"Good. In the meantime, I think we need to take a serious look into beefing up the security at the store. You can never be too safe."

"True but security only works if you use it. I left the door unlocked which made it easy for him to walk in."

I massaged my throbbing temples. A tension headache was stirring up just thinking about one more thing that needed to get done.

"You look stressed. Do you have time to take a quick little detour before we head back to the house? I want to show you something to help take your mind off things."

"Sure, why not."

He made a quick turn and within minutes pulled up to the boardwalk down the street from his renovation company.

"What's going on at the boardwalk?"

"Wait right there and I'll show you."

Cole walked around to the other side of the car and opened my door. I took his hand and followed his lead but was curious about where this little venture was leading to.

"Would you mind taking a trip down memory lane with me?"

"Sure."

He wrapped his arm around my shoulders.

"Come on, let's take a little stroll. I don't know if you recall but it was a little over a year ago that you met with me in my office. You came over to cancel the contract for your parents' renovations at the Inn, remember?"

"How could I forget?"

"I could tell you felt awful about having to cancel..." he said.

"Sooo, you made me make a deal with you to take a walk down to the creamery to get ice cream after the meeting."

"Yes! And it worked. We took a nice walk and it totally shifted the mood."

"And, if my memory serves me correctly, it was the first time you tried to ask me out on a date."

"I did, but you let me down... for good reasons of course. You were quite the honorable woman for wanting to make sure your sister's feelings wouldn't be hurt."

Just thinking back to that time made giggle. My youngest sister Rebecca had such a crush on Cole initially. All of that came to an end when mom called her out on it. Cole wasn't the right fit from the start but you couldn't tell Rebecca anything without some opposition.

"I'll admit that was crazy but thankfully we all survived. Now look at Rebecca. She's married and she's a mother. Who would've ever guessed all that could happen in just a little over a year's time?"

We stopped to look at the boats just like we did the last time we were here.

"You know, Cole, I really wanted to say yes to your invitation that day. But if you ever tell anyone, I promise I'll deny it."

"Your secret is safe with me. Besides, deep down I knew you couldn't resist all of this charm anyway."

"Oh yeah?"

I playfully whacked him in the arm with my purse.

"Okay, okay. Just kidding. Come here, let me make it up to you."

His soft kisses on my ear tickled me. Cole had such a playful way about him.

"Tickle me again and I'm pulling out the purse." I playfully threatened.

"Alright, in that case let's head inside the creamery."

I'm surprised we had room for ice cream with all the cake we sampled. Even if I couldn't finish it all, this spontaneous date was just what I needed.

HELEN

The family is coming over to celebrate Will's birthday in a little while and Payton was helping me to prepare the food. Having everyone over to the cottage was going to be very uplifting for Will and me, if only for a day. I was secretly starting to grow more weary at the thought of Payton leaving and having to take care of William on my own. She deserved to be married and happy, but with her gone, I would be the only one at the house to support Will as he continued to struggle with dementia.

"Mom, do you have any butter left?"

"There should be some on the left side of the fridge. If not, check the freezer. I always keep extra in there."

"You're the only person I know who freezes butter."

"That's what your grandmother used to do. I guess old habits die hard."

"Well, both of you are great cooks, so if it works for you, then it works for me, too."

"Mm hmm."

"You'll never guess who came into the store the other day."

"Mm hmm."

"Mom?"

"Yes, dear?"

"I said, you'll never guess who came into the store the other day. Are you okay? You seem a little distracted."

"I'm fine. Who came in the store?"

"Susan from high school. I haven't seen her since our girl's outing that went terribly wrong last year. Remember the way she spoiled everything for Abby by spreading gossip about her husband?"

"Mm hmm."

"Mom?"

"I'm listening to you."

"Okay, then what did I just say?"

"I heard you mention Susan's name."

"And?"

If I was being honest with myself I was a bit distracted.

"Mom, there's something on your mind and we're not going to lift one more utensil until you tell me what it is."

I placed everything down on the counter.

"I don't want to talk too loud and have your father overhear what we're saying. I know it's his birthday and all, but I've been thinking a lot about what our future is going to look like when you're gone."

"Ohh, mom your future is going to be just fine. I'll be close by, and so will Rebecca and Abby. "

"I know. It's the slow decline with Will and day to day functioning that worries me most. You've seen how persistent he's been in the past about not wanting a nurse around, but there are days where he forgets to change his clothes if I don't help him. We can't go on like this forever."

"Maybe it's time we take matters into our own hands and start looking into hiring someone to at least be here during the day. I really don't think dad will resist this time. Things have changed so much."

"I guess we can give it a try. I wouldn't put it past him to be resistant but you're right. We'll never know unless we try. The other thing I've been considering is whether or not it's time to put the cottage on the market."

"You want to sell the house?"

"I don't necessarily love the idea, but Payton, things are changing right before our very eyes. Will was always the one who kept this place up and running."

"What other options would you consider?"

"I haven't given it a lot of thought. Mainly because I don't want to think about it. The cottage has always been home for us. It holds so many fond memories. That corner over there is where you used to play school as a little girl while I was cooking. You would set up your chalk board and line up papers along the floor. I used to ask you what you were doing with all the papers and you would tell me it was for your students."

Payton smiled.

"I'm surprised I didn't turn out to be a teacher as much as I used to play school."

"That makes two of us. Then there was Abby who always wanted to play dress up. She must've thought you were her baby doll with the way she would dress you up and fix your hair."

"My how some things never change. She'd still do that today if I'd let her," Payton said.

"Ha! Didn't she try to give you a make-over as soon as you moved back from Connecticut?"

"She sure did. I think she missed her calling as a fashion guru or hair stylist."

"Perhaps. I guess what's weighing on my mind most are the memories of you, Abby, and Rebecca growing up here. Those memories have always been a part of me. Now you can see why I'm so torn with what to do."

"Mom, how about this. Let's take this whole thing one step at a time. We don't have to leap. For starters, let's look into having a nurse or an aide come to the house and help out. The rest of us can help with anything that has to do with regular maintenance around the house. We can evaluate things for a while, see how it's going, then take it from there."

Talking things over with Payton helped to ease my mind. Maybe I was jumping the gun but all I wanted was what was best for Will and the family.

"I guess that does make a lot of sense. I was starting to get myself all worked up without really thinking it through. Besides, we have so many happy things to focus on. Like your wedding shower coming up."

"I know. Can you believe it's that time already?"

"I can. Time waits for no one, my dear."

We continued baking and cooking up a storm and managed to finish just in time before everyone started walking through the door.

"Will, sweetheart, it's time to wake up." Begging Will to get up and get moving was a part time job in itself.

"Just a little while longer."

"Darlin, you should get up and go splash some water on your face. Everyone is here to celebrate your birthday."

"Birthday? What birthday?"

"Your 75th birthday, dear. Now come on, chop chop."

"Alright, alright."

I helped Will out of his chair and straightened up a bit. The kids really didn't care much about appearances anyway. What mattered most is soaking up every ounce of time together.

"Gram, Grandpa!" My grand-daughter Maggie ran over

and squeezed me tight. Her brother Aidan followed behind her.

"Ohh, my sweet grand-babies, give Gram a kiss."

Will gave the kids a pat and continued to shuffle his way to the bathroom. They knew their grandpa loved them and were very understanding.

"Hi, Mom." Abby and her husband Wyatt came over to give me hugs. They teased about missing all the extra attention from me since John William was born.

"Oh now, don't be silly. I have enough love to go around for everybody. Besides, these days I barely get away to see John William. Rebecca usually has to bring him over here to the house. Speaking of which, look who's here."

"Hi everybody!" Ethan waved as he held John William in his little carrier.

"Where's the man of the hour? I thought surely he'd be ready to party," Rebecca said.

"Your father is in the bathroom. He should be out in a minute."

Just then Will made his way back into the room to sit in his favorite chair.

"There he is. Happy seventy-fifth, Dad!" Rebecca came over and gave her dad a kiss. He nodded his head and went along with all the attention.

Payton was the first to scoop up baby John. She played with him and made him giggle and spit bubbles. Cole, Emmie, and Alice arrived just in time to watch him spit up all over Payton's blouse.

"That's okay little one. Come here. Let Gram clean you up."

"Gee, thanks, Mom. No, I don't need any help with my blouse, I'm fine." Payton teased.

"Oh, you'll be alright. You know where the wash cloths are kept."

It had been so long since we had a tiny little baby in the family, which made it very hard not to spoil John William.

"Payton, all jokes aside, I didn't realize you were so good with babies. After seeing you in action it kind of makes me think about having a little one of our own," Cole said.

Emmie was over the moon about the idea. "That would be so cool! Then I could finally be a big sister. I could feed the baby, give the baby a bath, and even read bedtime stories at night."

"I might be biased but I think Payton would make a wonderful mother. In a lot of ways Payton and Abby were a second mother to Rebecca when we were busy at the Inn," I said.

Rebecca agreed. "Oh, Payton you're a natural. Anytime you want to practice just come on over and hang out with John William. We could always use some extra help. Isn't that right, babe?"

"The more hands, the better!" Ethan added while tossing a few peanuts in his mouth.

"You two are funny. What are you going to do when you have two or three kids running around the house?" I was assuming they would want more kids but Rebecca was always unpredictable growing up. That really hasn't changed in her adult years.

"Mom, don't get too excited about the idea of me having three kids. Pushing out the first one was almost too much to bear."

"Don't say that. Giving birth may have been difficult but having this precious baby boy in our lives was well worth it."

"I don't disagree but for now we're all here to celebrate dad. And, I don't know about you guys but I'm hungry!"

"Way to change the subject, Becks!" Payton tugged on her ponytail.

We all made ourselves comfortable and spread out between the dining room and the living room to eat and talk. Alice kept me company in the kitchen as we prepared the second round of plates for dessert.

"So, Alice, is there a reason why you didn't bring Stanley with you? I was hoping we would get to meet him."

"I didn't know I could bring a plus one. Don't worry. You'll meet him soon enough. I'm bringing him to the wedding."

"Really! I can't wait to meet him. I'm assuming things went very well after we last spoke?"

"They did. We had a chance to talk and I gained a lot of insight about his feelings and past experiences. It was a good conversation. I guess I can officially say that he's more than just a friend."

Cole walked into the kitchen just in time to hear her confession.

"Who's more than just a friend?" he asked.

"Well, Son, I was going to wait and talk about this later on but I guess now is just as good of a time as any. Stanley and I are seeing each other."

"You mean the old guy that comes over for tea every week?"

"Cole! The old guy has a name. Do you have to be so rude about it?"

"I'm not trying to be rude. I just thought he was an old friend. You're the one that made light of it when we talked about this a while back. How was I supposed to know?"

"I'm not saying you had to know anything but you don't have to make him sound like an old prune. And, to clear things up, we were friends. Now, we're more than friends."

"Okayyyy, well, I guess I would know these things and have a chance to actually meet the guy if you lived closer."

"Cole, I only live forty minutes away and I don't plan on moving any time soon. If you guys want to move closer to me you're more than welcome."

"Now, now you two. I've never known the Millers to be at odds. Cole, take it from me when I say that even us more mature adults deserve to be happy and to have a love life," I said.

Alice nodded her head in agreement. I didn't want to discourage Cole but it was true. Everybody deserved to be happy and find love if that's what they really wanted.

"Don't you want to see your mother happy?"

"Of course I do, but I don't ever want to see anybody take advantage of her, that's all."

He turned toward Alice to speak.

"Mom, if Stanley makes you happy, then I'm happy. Just text me his address in case he messes up and I need to come looking for him."

We all laughed at the thought. Cole was a good man and had nothing but the best in mind for his mother, Emmie, and Payton as his future wife.

Abby lit the candles on Will's cake.

"Alright, everybody. Now that we've settled on Stanley being an accepted friend of the family, why don't we all go in the living room and sing happy birthday to dad," she said.

One by one we piled into the living room and gathered around Will. Abby protected the small flames and led us all in the traditional birthday song.

"Okay, Dad, on the count of three blow out the candles. One... two... three..."

Will blew out the candles and we all showered him with all the love and attention that he could handle. He didn't say much but I believe that even Will's spirit was uplifted by being surrounded by family.

~

Later that evening we brewed a pot of coffee and hung out in the kitchen.

"Payton, didn't you mention something about running into Susan earlier?" I asked.

"Oh, yeah, I almost forgot. She came into the store earlier this week."

"Really? What did she want?" Abby perked up.

"She actually came in to show support to the business and apologize for what she did last summer." Payton's voice dwindled.

"Apologize to who? You? Payton, you can't be serious! She must be confused. It was my marriage that she almost tried to sabotage."

"Abby, hold on a second. Let me explain before you get all bent out of shape."

"Okay, go on, I'm listening."

"She said that she owes us all an apology, Abby. Not just you. You were impacted the most by what she said but she ruined the day for all of us. She said she has every intention of reaching out to you as well."

"Nonsense. If she was so sorry, why are we just now having this conversation almost a year later? Give me a break! You can go back and tell her that I'm a grown woman with kids and I don't have time to play her foolish games."

"Wow, I don't know who this Susan is but she doesn't sound like anybody I'd want to be friends with," Alice said.

"Thank you, Alice," Abby said.

"Ladies, you may not agree but here's the way I see it. Was Susan wrong for repeating false rumors? Yes! There's no question about it. But, you've known her long enough to know she wouldn't personally do anything to hurt you. It's water under the bridge now. Let's forget about it and move on." I stopped to give my attention to my grandkids as they came running toward me.

"Gram, can Emmie, Aidan, and I have some ice cream and another piece of cake?" Maggie said.

"More ice cream and cake? My my, I didn't know little girls and boys had so much room in their tummies."

"Oh, no, you two. If Emmie's dad approves that's fine, but you two little munchkins have had enough." Abby wasn't falling for it. She knew it would be a long night filled with tummy aches if I gave in to their request. They quickly disappeared from the kitchen.

"Mom, with regard to Susan, I love your ability to look for the silver lining in this situation, I really do. But, trust me when I tell you that what she said was intentional."

Payton interjected.

"Abby, maybe at the time but I believe she's sincere now. I haven't finished telling you everything. It actually gets worse."

I took a few sips of coffee and continued to listen.

"She admitted that she was the one having real marital problems with her husband. When we saw her last summer her husband had already moved out and they were on their way to getting a divorce."

"So, because Susan was down on her luck she was going to try and drag Abby into it as well?" Rebecca said.

"Rebecca, she didn't say that. She just admitted that she was wrong for repeating the rumor about Abby's husband. But get this...when I asked her why they were getting a divorce, she told me there was infidelity involved. I felt so bad and commented that I felt sorry for her. She said she probably deserved it since she was the one who cheated."

"Wait, what?"Abby put her coffee down.

Rebecca was even more stunned by the news. "Hold on.

She not only laid up on that beach chair and tried to make Abby feel uncomfortable over false rumors about Wyatt, but the whole time she was creeping around behind her husband's back?"

"Yup."

"That low down and dirty little..." Rebecca murmured under her breath.

"Uhh, that will be all, Rebecca. Whatever she's going through in her marriage is her business." I tried to be the voice of reason.

Payton protested. "Mom, she shared all of this with me, not the other way around."

"That's fine, but we don't have to judge. It actually explains why she feels the need to apologize to everyone. The poor thing has probably been carrying the guilt and weight of everything on her shoulders and can't take it anymore."

"Poor thing?" Abby waved her hand in disgust.

"I don't get how she becomes the victim. Did I miss something here?"

"Abby, you didn't miss anything! I know what it's like to be in her shoes. And, I don't think it's fair for you to pass judgement, that's all."

As soon as the words slipped out of my mouth I immediately regretted getting involved in the conversation. I let my emotions get the best of me. The girls looked stunned and Alice looked like she was trying to bury her nose in her coffee mug.

"Don't just stand there and stare. You heard me right. I know first hand what it's like to carry the guilt and shame that comes along with stepping outside of a marriage. It's nothing that I'm proud of. Your father and I always withheld this part of our marriage from you girls because we didn't want you to be dragged into the hurt and pain associated with it. I can't speak for Susan but I knew I was wrong for what I did. And, the last thing I needed was judgement from anybody. The guilt and shame was enough punishment in itself. We lived through that over thirty years ago but I remember the pain like it was yesterday. Back then, word spread around town so fast it made my head spin. I could live with the embarrassment but I couldn't bear what I put your father through. Thankfully, he eventually came around to forgiving me. And, despite whatever you may be thinking of me now, if it wasn't for your father's forgiveness, we may not be the close knit family that we are today."

"Wow. It seems like this town has had its fair share of..." Payton's voice trailed off before completing the sentence.

"I'm sorry. I didn't mean any harm, Mom. You know that we love you. There's not one person in this room who's perfect. Not one."

"Thank you, Payton, but I'm not looking for empathy. I just hope we can be the kind of women that learn how to walk a mile in somebody else's shoes before we cast judgement. What Susan said to Abby was hurtful but it's not beyond repair. Do as you please, but I'd rather offer forgiveness and squash it. Someday you might actually need forgiveness in return."

Payton rested her head on my shoulder. I'm sure the girls will never forget the day that I revealed my darkest secret. But, what I hope they gained from it was the importance of forgiveness. My mother used to tell us life was way too short to get caught up in the weeds.

PAYTON

"Natalie, please empty everything out of your pockets and place it on the counter."

She jumped at the sound of my voice and dropped a few singles out of her hand.

"Payton, I was just... I was just checking the drawer count. I swear I..."

"It's only an hour into your shift. We don't check the count until the end of the day. Empty your pockets."

"I can explain."

"Natalie."

A hundred dollar bill and a few twenties were in her front pockets. She even managed to stuff more money in her back pockets.

I walked over and collected the money and proceeded to count what was there.

"Is that all or do I need to ask you to empty your book bag as well?"

"That's all. I swear I didn't take anything else. I'll empty out my bag for you right now. Whatever you do, please don't fire me."

Her eyes welled up with tears.

"I can explain, Payton."

"I can't think of one good reason why I shouldn't fire you right here on the spot. I trusted you, Natalie."

In between sniffles she began to explain.

"I know what I was doing was wrong but I really am a good kid. I promise I am."

"That's just it. You're not a kid. You're over eighteen years of age. I could report this to the police."

"Please don't. Please let me explain. Mom is really sick. She was recently laid off because she's not able to perform her duties. It was contract work to begin with but within six months, as long as they liked her, the position would become full time. She's trying so hard but the only income we have right now is her unemployment and my paycheck from this job. This job is all I have."

I relaxed on the counter and let out a deep breath.

"Why didn't you just say something to me, Natalie? We could've sat down and brainstormed together. I was looking to increase your hours when you returned anyway. It may not solve all your problems but it could've helped."

"I don't know. I guess I just felt embarrassed to unload all of my personal problems here at work. It feels like everything is going wrong all at once."

"Is there something else?" I asked.

"I had to drop out of school because we were getting behind in payments."

"But, it's your last semester. Can't they work with you?"

"They already have been working with us. That's one of the reasons why I applied for this job, so I could supplement and help out with my school bills. The money runs out pretty quickly when you don't really have enough to begin with."

"Which explains why you were trying to steal from the cash register."

Natalie held her head down.

"Yes."

"I'm not sure that one hundred and sixty-five dollars would've solved much, Natalie. I worked hard to get this place up and running. Maybe you view me as some wealthy woman who wouldn't miss a few nickels and dimes but that's not the case. I have to pay my monthly rent to the landlord to keep this store open. And, until I'm married I still live at home with my folks to save money."

"I'm sorry, I didn't know."

"You shouldn't have to know. You should just want to do the right thing, Natalie. Period."

She nodded her head while stifling her cry. I felt like she was being sincere but she needed to know that stealing would not be tolerated.

"Look. I'm not going to sit here and pretend like I haven't made some wrong choices in my past. We all have. I just can't have you working here with me if I can't trust you."

"I don't blame you for wanting to fire me, Payton. What I did was really rotten. I'll get my things."

I felt torn. Deep down she really was just a kid with the weight of the world on her shoulders.

"Natalie, wait."

She turned around and barely whispered.

"Yes."

"I want you to stay just as much as you want to be here. But, I need to know that I can count on you to be honest with me."

"Oh, Payton, I promise you won't have any more trouble out of me."

"I know I won't. I believe you've learned your lesson. Besides, I was already going to have security cameras installed for security reasons. If anything like this happens again, it's on you!"

"Yes, ma'am. I promise."

I passed her the tissue box.

"You've been talking about your mother being sick for a while now. If you don't mind me asking, what's wrong with her?"

"We don't know. Neither one of us has health insurance. We paid out of pocket at the beginning of the year for a doctor's visit but they wanted us to go have testing. We barely could afford that visit so testing was definitely out of the question."

Again I sighed. I know I was supposed to maintain a fine line between professional and personal but it was hard not to be touched by their situation.

"Well, look, Natalie. I wish I had the answers to completely solve everything but, unfortunately, I don't. The only thing I do have to offer, if you're interested, is a full time job."

"If I'm interested? Are you kidding?"

Natalie began to break down in tears again. Her eyes were puffy and her nose was red. If a customer walked in they would surely think that I did something to her.

"Don't cry. I'm trying to help, not make it worse. Don't get me wrong, we will both benefit from this. I wouldn't be paying you full time to do nothing but..."

"You are helping me, Payton. Even when I don't deserve it. I don't even know what to say."

"You don't have to say anything. With the wedding coming up, my honeymoon, and even after I return, I need extra help around here. It seems like not long after you helped me with building my online presence all of a sudden things really started picking up. That goes to show how much the business has changed over time."

Natalie laughed.

"That's how much our world has changed over time. Technology is everything."

"I get it, but I'm old school, and having you here has taught me to get with the times. Funny thing is I always thought I was pretty hip as a woman approaching her mid forties. I guess I have some catching up to do."

We exchanged a smile which helped Natalie to finally stop crying and relax.

"Natalie, this won't last forever. You and your mother will get back on your feet again. And, the day will come where you will get back to finishing your degree and pursuing your dreams again."

"I guess."

"I know it doesn't feel like it but you'll be fine. Trouble doesn't last forever. In the meantime, where's that boyfriend of yours? Is he being supportive and understanding?"

"We broke up."

"Aww, Natalie, I'm sorry."

"Don't be. I had to focus my attention on mom. I guess it's hard to keep a boyfriend if you can't spend time with him."

"If he's going to take off and leave you when you're down on your luck, you don't need him anyway. You can do better. You're beautiful, smart, and caring. If he couldn't see that then let him be on his way."

"Mom says it was his loss."

"I like the way your mother thinks. Listen, why don't you take a five minute break and clean up your face. With all that mascara running down your face the customers are going to think I abused you."

"Okay."

"When you get back we can talk about your new schedule."

"Sounds good. Hey, Payton..."

"Yes?"

"Thank you... for everything."

Natalie humbly lowered her head and walked to the back room. Going forward I'd keep an eye out to make sure she was keeping her word, but deep down inside I knew everything was going to be just fine.

~

Later that evening Emmie and I went to the diner for milkshakes.

"So, are you getting excited about being a bridesmaid?"

She nodded while slurping on her strawberry shake.

"Yep. I even cut down on my regular shakes so I could make sure my dress still fits."

"Emmie, are you serious? You cut down on your shake intake for me?"

"Mm hmm."

"Well, that's sweet of you but you're so tiny I doubt that an occasional shake will change that. Now, when you get to be my age, then we can talk."

"You sound like grandma. She said the same thing."

"It's true!"

"Hey, Payton."

"Yes?"

"Since it's just the two of us here do you think we could have girl talk?"

"I was hoping we could. Do you have anything in particular on your mind?"

"Kinda. It's something dad said we should talk about during our alone time."

"You can tell me anything, Emmie. What's up?"

"Now that you and dad are getting married, I was wondering what I should call you?"

"I see...well, this is a very important topic. I think you should start by listening to your heart."

"What do you mean?"

"Don't answer this question out loud. Just think about it for a minute. What's in your heart? What do you want to call me?"

"You mean you're not going to tell me what I should call you?"

"No. I think this should be something that comes from your heart and something we can all agree on together."

The biggest smile emerged from Emmie's face.

"When I'm with my friends, they call their mothers mom all the time. I don't know what that's like. I can't remember my mother. All I have are the stories that dad tells me and lots of pictures. If my real mom is watching us from heaven, I don't think she would mind if I called you mom, too."

I tried to keep my composure in front of Emmie but that was the sweetest thing anyone had ever said to me.

"Emmie, I'd be honored to have you call me mom. If that's what would make you happy, then it makes me happy, too. I hope you know that I would never try and take the place of your real mom. Instead, I will love you and help you keep her memory alive."

"Thanks."

"Anything for you, Emms. Is there anything else on your mind?"

"Well, since you asked..." she said with a smirk on her face.

"Uh oh, I smell trouble."

"Not really, I just need some advice."

"Oh, okay. What's up?"

"My friends have been talking to me about starting sixth grade in August and it's making me a little nervous."

"Already? It's only June. What could you possibly be nervous about?"

"I heard from my friend Montana that in sixth grade the boys start to like you. She said they either like you or they tease you. All the boys around here are disgusting and I don't want them to bother me."

She flipped her hair to the side. I could tell she was passionate about it so I tried to recall what I would've done in middle school.

"How does Montana know so much about middle school if she was in fifth grade with you this year?"

"Her older sister tells her everything about middle school."

"I see. Well, I would say be careful not to get yourself all worked up about something that hasn't happened yet. Maybe Montana's older sister had that experience and you won't. Besides, all you have to focus on is surrounding yourself with a circle of sweet friends. That's what I did in middle school and it worked out pretty well for me."

"So, no one ever teased you?"

"They tried every now and again but my older sister and my friends wouldn't stand for it."

I leaned over to whisper some additional words of wisdom.

"Trust me. Start working on building your sweet team from the beginning. That way you can all look out for each other."

"That's a good idea. I'm sure I'll meet somebody I can be friends with."

"That's the spirit. You're going to do great in middle school. Oh, there's one more thing that you have to do and it's super important!"

"What's that?"

"When you see someone who's sitting all by themselves and it looks like they're in need of a friend..."

"Wait, I already know what you're going to say... invite them to join my sweet team, right?"

"You got it! See, you're a natural, Emmie. I wouldn't be too worried about middle school at all. As for the boys, they're so worried about not looking dorky in front of their friends, you won't have to worry about them."

"Dorky?" Emmie looked confused.

"Yeah, you know, like a goofball. How do you and your friends say it?"

"We just say they look dumb."

"Or that. Either way you get the idea. Now, what do you say we order a shake to go for your dad?"

"He's going to love that. Give him a chocolate shake and he'll be the happiest man on the whole planet."

"One chocolate shake coming right up!"

REBECCA

"Alright everybody, this next game is sure to spice things up. If anyone mentions one of the following words, you get to take a clothes pin away from them. The one who ends up with the most pins in the end wins the game. Are you ready?"

About thirty women were standing around the room with clothes pins attached to their garments. We had all played different versions of the classic baby and bridal shower games. Each time we played we managed to rise to the occasion and make it fun all over again.

"Okay, here we go. The words are wedding, honeymoon, dress, bride, and shoes. Remember, if you say any of the words I just mentioned, you'll have to give up a pin."

"Five words? Since when did they change the rules to the game? I barely can keep up with one word and now you want me to keep from saying five? Good night of living! Who wants my pins? I'm out." Daddy's cousin Jolene drove in for the shower from Jacksonville. We didn't see her very often but when she did come around we were sure to be entertained or embarrassed.

"Jolene, don't be a party pooper. Come sit with me. I'll show you how it's done," mom offered.

"Helen, I'll watch you while I sip on something to help relax my nerves. The drive from Jacksonville nearly put me out of commission. I'm getting too old to be running up and down the road. Plus these shoes hurt so bad I..."

"Cousin Jolene, hand over your pin!" I said.

"What's that now?"

"You have to hand over your pin. You said shoes."

"That's because these bunions are giving me a fit. Now go on and chase after somebody else. Shoo! And, don't come back until you have that sweet baby boy of yours so I can meet him."

Cousin Jolene was as sassy as they come and didn't have a filter. At least if she had one she never used it.

"Rebecca and Abby, I can't thank you enough for organizing my shower. Everything is perfect. The guests, the games, and the venue of all places! How in the world did you manage to pull off a shower at Marina Del Mar? This place was booked for the entire summer," Payton said.

Abby leaned in. "Trust me, we had to pull a lot of major strings. Our back up location would've been mom and dad's house if we couldn't pull it off."

"She's not kidding. We literally have to get out of here on time so they can prepare for a reception right after," I added.

"Wow, thank you for doing this. The shower couldn't be more perfect."

We were surrounded by a panoramic view of the ocean, which made for a beautiful backdrop as we mingled. Payton was beaming from ear to ear which made it all worthwhile.

Emmie ran over to Payton. You could tell she was excited about presenting something special in a large white box.

"I have a gift for you." Emmie presented a box to Payton.

"It's from grandma and me. She said I should put it on the table with the other gifts, but I really think you should open it now."

"You know what, Emmie, that's not a bad idea. Why don't we bring Payton over to the bridal chair so she can open all of her gifts," I offered.

I tapped a glass to get everyone's attention.

"Ladies..."

"Oh, no. Not another game." Cousin Jolene sat a few feet away but spoke loud enough to be heard across the room.

"Ladies, may I have your attention? I can see that many of you are doing well with collecting pins. At this time we're going to gather by the bridal chair decorated by yours truly. Payton, if you will have a seat we can begin passing you the gifts."

"Looks like Rebecca picked up a few pounds in the rear end after having the baby."

I could hear Jolene in the background talking so loud one would've thought she was hard of hearing.

"Cousin Jolennnne...we cannn hearrrr youuuu!" I tried to be pleasant. I normally didn't do polite but I was trying not to make a scene at Payton's shower.

"Abby, why don't you take over and help with the gifts. I need to go find a bottle of wine."

"That's the spirit. Bring me one, too!" Cousin Jolene chimed in.

I rolled my eyes but no one could really see me except Abby.

"Rebecca, it's twelve o'clock in the afternoon. Nobody is having a bottle of anything. Now, stay here and help... and for goodness sake, smile!"

I whispered to Abby while I bent over to pick up the next gift.

"I was smiling until Cousin Jolene showed up. She told mom that I gained weight after having John William."

"And? What's the problem? You still look good, Rebecca. I don't understand why you're letting Jolene, of all people, get under your skin. You know the woman isn't dealing with a full deck to begin with."

Payton stood to give Emmie and Alice a hug for the dinnerware set and engraved glass pitcher.

"Thank you, Emmie... thanks, Alice. Your gift will definitely be put to good use."

"There's more where that came from. You're going to need it. Cole has a bachelor's kitchen that needs a woman's touch," Alice said.

Abby passed the next gift along to Payton while I wrote down who it was from. I was still irritated.

"Abby, I don't agree with what you said one bit. I think she is dealing with a full deck. She's just arrived at the age where she says whatever's on her mind without a filter, that's all."

"Nope. I don't believe it. She's done way too many things over the years that justify being a little cray cray."

I continued collecting wrapping paper in between recording gifts. Payton was giving us the side eye but Abby didn't notice. She continued whispering as she passed along the next gift.

"Remember the summer we went to her house by the lake? I don't think she let the sun rise good before she was out back targeting beer cans with her shot gun," Abby said.

"Oh, yeah. I almost forgot about that. We nearly jumped right out of our skin. I bet nobody went back to sleep that morning."

"You mean every morning the entire time we were out there. And, when we finally worked up the nerve to ask her about it she said it was her morning ritual before heading off to work. Imagine that!"

"I'm surprised the neighbors didn't report her for breaking the local ordinance," I said.

"I don't think there is such a thing when you live out in the back woods."

"Will you two hush!" Payton looked annoyed.

"Sorry," I whispered.

Afterward, we ate cake and mingled for a while longer.

"What has gotten into you two?" mom asked.

"Don't look at me. Rebecca is the one who's annoyed at Cousin Jolene," Abby said.

"Abby, you were talking about her just as much as I was."

"What for?" Mom stood there looking as if she didn't know how special Jolene was.

"We were just discussing how she's... you know...outspoken... rude..."

"Crazy," Abby added.

"I beg your pardon. Jolene has a unique way about her but she's family."

"She can still be family and be crazy," Abby said.

Mom cut a look toward Abby.

"You two oughta be ashamed. I'm really surprised at you, Abby."

"Abby? You're surprised at Abby? In our defense, Jolene came in here smelling like she fell off the wagon, talking out loud about her bunions, and how I gained weight in my rear end, but you're scolding us? I thought we were all classier than that."

"Look, Jolene is a very well respected woman in her home town. She carried the title of nurse but performed her duties to the caliber of a doctor. She's well known in her community and was held to the highest esteem. After her husband's passing things changed tremendously for her. Times are a little bit harder for her now. But that shouldn't matter. She's still family. So try and be kind and cut her some slack."

"I'll behave for you, but I'm glad she's heading back home after the shower," I said.

Mom stood quietly for a moment. "About that. I was thinking it might be nice if Jolene came and stayed with us for a little while," she said.

"Mom, have you lost your mind?"

"No! I'm being serious, Rebecca."

"So am I!"

"Since things have been pretty tough on her lately, I was thinking it might be a win-win situation for both of us. She's trying to get rid of her house to relieve her finances and we need a nurse for your father. She's experienced and she's a trusted member of the family."

"Okay, I see where you're trying to go with this but having Jolene come to a bridal shower, verses having Jolene come live with you is two different things," Abby said.

"Abby, you're making a snap judgement without thinking this through."

"Mom, I could say the same. You haven't seen Jolene in ages and now you want her to come live with you?"

"I'm trying to consider your father. Jolene is his cousin. I think he'd be less resistant to the idea of someone coming to help if it was family."

"We can discuss this later when everyone has had a chance to think it through." No one ever listened to the youngest in my family but I thought I'd try just the same.

Mom smoothed out her clothing and held her head up high. "There's nothing to discuss. The decision has already been made. In a few weeks when Payton moves out, Jolene will be moving in."

Abby looked shocked. "Ok, please tell me this is a joke? Don't you think we should all talk this over first?"

"Why? Last time I checked you have two little children at home to care for, Abby. Rebecca has a newborn, and Payton will be a newlywed with a child of her own to look after. I've been crying out for months now saying that your father's dementia is getting worse. Now, I finally have a solution, and whether you like it or not, Jolene is coming to live with us. Case closed."

There was no point in pushing the envelope. Abby looked annoyed and mom seemed to have her mind made up. Just as I turned around to head back to the party I bumped right into Payton.

"Can you three please kindly tell me what's going on? I thought we were all here to celebrate my wedding but all you can seem to do is bicker with one another."

"Somebody said the word wedding! You better hand over the pin before Rebecca gets after you."

Jolene yelled from a few feet away.

"So, who's going to tell me what's going on?"

"Nothing is going on. We were all about to join the party before you came walking this way." Abby tried her best to clean things up but Payton wasn't going for it.

"Nonsense, Abby and Rebecca carried on with each other the whole time I was opening my gifts, and now mom is involved. What's...going...on?"

Since I had the reputation for always being the trouble-maker I figured why stop now.

"Mom asked Cousin Jolene to come live with her and daddy when you move," I blurted out.

"Rebecca! Was that necessary?" Mom was ticked.

"Somebody had to tell her."

Payton faced mom. "Cousin Jolene?" she asked.

"Yes, Cousin Jolene. And, before you give me the third degree, I'm going to tell you just like I told your sisters, she's family. And, having family around beats dealing with a stranger. Period. End of story."

"But what about us? We're all here to help you."

"Payton, I don't doubt for one minute that you'll all be around. But we need around the clock care. All of you need to be there for your husbands and your children."

"I think you're letting fear lead you on this one, Mom. But, who am I to try and influence you? I just hope you aren't going to regret your decision. Jolene can be even more of a handful than daddy. There's a reason why she lives miles away and we rarely see her."

Payton didn't realize while she was talking that Jolene had walked up behind her. I tried to warn her but she wasn't picking up on my signals.

"Payton..." Jolene had a stern look on her face. She stood a little over five feet tall, wore her hair cut short with a straw hat and dressed like something out of the 1980s.

"Cousin Jolene, I... I didn't see you there."

"How could you with your back turned? I just wanted to stop by and give you my well wishes before heading back to the hotel."

Mom tried to stop Jolene from leaving.

"Jolene, you haven't been here that long. Is everything alright?"

"Everything is fine. I just need to rest these old bones of mine. It probably wasn't a good idea that I tried to drive here on the same day as the shower."

"Well, you know you can stay at the house, Jolene. You don't have to waste your money at a hotel."

"I know, but don't you worry. They'll be plenty of time for

us to be under the same roof, Helen. Plenty of time." She started walking out of the door before turning around.

"Besides, it seems like your daughters need some time to get used to the idea." She turned to leave but yelled over her shoulder...

"Let it sink in, ladies...Cousin Jolene is coming to Pelican Beach!"

The glass doors closed behind her. The women at the shower tried to act nonchalant but let's face it, Jolene had already made her presence known. For the next few weeks I'm certain Payton's shower would be the talk of the town.

PAYTON

"Slide to the left and slide to the right and slowly dip her back. Nice job... from the top. Slide to the left... slide to the right... and slowly dip her back."

Our bodies glided in unison as we followed the lead of our dance instructor. It was our last session and we had made great strides in preparation for our big day.

"Cole and Payton, you did a wonderful job today. My next client won't be here for another hour. You're more than welcome to use the studio for a little longer if you'd like."

Cole extended his hand toward me.

"What do you say? One more dance before we hit the road?"

"Sure."

Our instructor left the music playing and I rested my head on Cole's shoulder. If I could close my eyes and dance forever in his arms that still wouldn't be long enough.

"Do you think we're ready to hit the dance floor this Saturday?" He stroked the back of my head while swaying to the music.

"I don't see why not. We've been practicing with the best. As long as I have you by my side that's all that matters to me."

"Alright, but if I stumble and trip over my own feet I just need to know you're prepared to catch me. Remember, out of the two of us, I'm the one with the two left feet."

"I'll catch you, babe."

We continued to sway and sneak in a few sweet kisses on the dance floor.

"You know, I was just thinking... I can't believe the wedding is finally here. It seems like the journey we traveled to get here has been tremendous."

He kissed me on the forehead before asking, "What do you mean?"

"Think about it, since you proposed so much has happened. Rebecca and Ethan surprised the family with John William, you broke your leg earlier in the year, your mom fell in love..."

"Hey, hey...he's just a boyfriend. Let's not rush things."

I thought it was funny the way Cole always displayed his protective side when it came to his mother's heart.

"You get the idea. It's been quite the year and those were just the highlights."

"It sure has been quite the year. I had to sit through two rounds of cake tasting with you. If someone would've told me that my future wife was going to scream and holler over blue velvet cake I would've requested it right from the start."

"Oh, man! I'll admit I was being picky...but that cake...oh it's to die for! And, it's nothing like what I initially wanted. We'll have to save some from the wedding and freeze it to eat on our anniversary."

Cole's smile started to fade as the song began to end.

"What is it, babe?"

"It's nothing."

"No, it's something alright. Tell me what's on your mind."

"I just thought about one of the low moments from the year... for me that would be when Jack showed up."

"I almost forgot about that. You don't have anything to worry about, Cole. Jack is a thing of the past. I think he received the message loud and clear."

"Let's hope so."

While I yelled to thank Amanda, Cole picked me up and carried me out of the studio.

"What would you say if you saw two love birds parked on the beach and relaxing in each others arms?"

"I'd saaay.. they're pretty lucky to be so in love. Why? Do you know two love birds who fit the description?"

"I sure do!"

He put me down and opened the door to his truck.

"Let me guess. Are we heading to the beach?"

"That's for me to know and you to find out."

Before long Cole was backing his pickup through the public access entry to Pelican Beach. The sun had set and we probably had no business driving out here after hours. But, my man didn't care. We were about to commit to a lifetime together and that's all that mattered.

"I'll meet you at the back of the truck." He smiled like he was up to something.

"Cole Miller, I'm a respectable woman and I will not be caught in public frolicking around the back of your..."

"Payton, I meant so we can sit up and watch the stars."

"Oh... ha ha...just kidding."

"I got your ha ha." He teased.

"Come on, last one to the back of the truck is a rotten egg."

He pulled out a lightweight blanket and a cooler and set everything up just so.

"Cole, you are so thoughtful. When did you have time to plan all this?"

"I pulled it together not long before I picked you up this evening. I figured it might be nice to squeeze in one last date before we officially become Mr. and Mrs. Miller."

"I love you, Cole."

"I love you, too."

He planted a loving kiss on my forehead and then reached for two glasses.

"I know this seems a little cheesy but I decided to go with cider, grapes, cheese, crackers, and deli rolls."

"I don't think it's cheesy at all. I think it's thoughtful and romantic."

"You sure? We can always go grab something else if you want to."

"And miss out on this romantic scenery? No way."

Cole leaned back and rested against the cabin while eating his grapes.

"I was just thinking... imagine what life would be like if you weren't at the Inn the day we met."

"I guess we would've carried on with life as usual not realizing what we were missing."

"Yeah, I guess. It just reminds me that everything happens for a reason."

"It sure does. I hadn't been back here long when we met but I was on a mission. I was listing all the sites in the Pelican Beach area where I could take clients for photoshoots. Although, I only had freelance work in mind at the time. I had no idea I'd actually open up a store. The store came under your influence!"

"Are you still happy with the decision?"

"For the most part, I'd say so. Sometimes I miss just being a free spirit but overall, I think it's better to have a presence in the community."

"Well, if you ever want to go back to freelance work I'll support you, or if you decide you want to expand the store, I'll support you with that, too!"

"Aww, thanks, babe. I was thinking I'd give it another year, and if things continue to go well, I'm going to make the landlord an offer to buy the store. Natalie's been wonderful about helping me to build my online presence and I'm pretty certain it will continue to grow."

"I haven't heard you mention her name in a while. I guess everything is going well with her."

I hesitated to get too deep with work talk on what was supposed to be a romantic evening. Besides, I knew if I went into all the details from the stealing incident, Cole might not approve of my decision to keep her as an employee.

"Things are going fairly well. I recently increased her hours to full time. I could really use the extra help and since her mother has been really sick, I'm hoping it will help with their financial situation."

"Payton, that's sweet of you and all... but did you offer her the job because you really need the help and can afford it? Or do you feel sorry for her?"

"I knew you would say that. Don't worry, I promise we can afford it and her help is very much needed. Now, enough about work. I could've sworn you were just about to come a little closer and hold me."

"I sure was. Come here, beautiful."

PAYTON

"Payton and Cole, the wedding is absolutely amazing, and darling, your dress looks stunning. Simply stunning!"

"Thank you, Alice. Of course, I have sweet Emmie to thank for finding it for me."

Emmie blushed as I put her in the spotlight. She made the whole family proud today as she stood with my sisters as a bridesmaid. The bridesmaids wore silk mauve dresses that looked lovely with the men's light gray suits.

"Come here you two. Let me give you a hug. I wish you only the best as you begin this new chapter as husband and wife."

"Thanks, Mom," Cole said.

A gentleman walked up and joined Alice by her side.

"There you are. Perfect timing. Cole... Payton... I'd like for you to officially meet Stanley."

Cole extended his hand and gave him a firm hand shake.

"Yes, that's right. You did mention you were bringing a plus one to the wedding. Stanley, nice to meet you."

Stanley wore a navy blue tie to match Alice's dress. They made a lovely looking couple.

"It's nice to finally meet you, Payton and Cole. I've heard so much about you. I've also heard a lot about this young lady over here..."

Emmie extended her hand.

"Hi, I'm Emmie. Are you grandma's new boyfriend?"

Stanley smiled at Alice first, before responding.

"Well, I guess we are going steady, aren't we, Alice?"

"Where are you going?" Emmie asked out of confusion.

"We're staying right here, darlin. Come on, let's go introduce Stanley to our friends and family, and let your parents mingle with their guests."

"Grown ups are so confusing." Emmie's facial expression was priceless.

"Alice, you and Emmie go ahead. I'll be right behind you."

"Okay, come on, Emmie."

Stanley turned to address Cole.

"Hey, uh, I know you probably have some reservations about me, Cole. If I were in your shoes I'd also want to know who's spending time with my mother. When you have time after the wedding I'd like for all of us to get together and spend time getting to know each other better. I think you'll be pleasantly surprised to know that I'm one of the good ones and I have nothing but good intensions."

He gave Cole a pat on the arm, wished us both well, and then walked away.

"He seems like a nice man," I said.

"So far. We'll see."

"Ohh, Cole. Stop being so silly. Let your mother live her life."

"I will... I will. Hey, enough about him. You look like you

belong on the cover of a magazine. I'm so proud to call you my wife."

Cole nuzzled his nose against mine.

"Alright you two. They'll be plenty of time for all that later on. Stand together here with your sisters, and Helen, and William. I want to take a group picture." Cousin Jolene returned this week and promised to be on her best behavior for the wedding.

"Helen, pull Will closer to you. Closer... closer...that's it! Alright, now we need the husbands and the kids to join in. Rebecca and Abby, call your husbands and kids. There's so many of them running around here I don't know which one belongs to who."

"Cousin Jolene, you know we already have a professional photographer taking photos, right?"

"Payton, you know better than everybody else how long it takes for those pictures to arrive. Now smile!"

The husbands joined in with my niece and nephews and took the most disorganized photos imaginable. But, for the sake of keeping Cousin Jolene happy we all went along with the photo.

"Thank you, everybody, that'll be all. Now which one of these waiters is going to help me find a glass of brandy on the rocks?"

She walked off determined to flag down a waiter.

"Good Lord, does she ever take it easy? How about a club soda, Cousin Jolene." Rebecca followed behind her to try and do a little damage control.

"Mom... Abby... come here for a second. How does everything look? Do you think the guests are enjoying themselves?"

"Everything looks wonderful and everyone is having a fabulous time. What are you worried about?" Abby said.

"It really does, Payton. The crew that you hired is doing a

top notch job. Valet is running smoothly, the tables look gorgeous, the tents are beautiful, even the dance floor, for goodness sake. I don't know how you pulled it all off," Mom said.

"Really? Okay, I just want everything to be perfect for the guests."

"Payton, it's your special day. Relax and enjoy it. You and Cole have literally created a romantic beach getaway for your wedding, I think they'll be just fine."

"Thanks, Ab."

"Speaking of Cole, here's my son-in-law now." Mom spread her arms wide and made such a fuss over Cole. She was tickled pink that our union had finally come to fruition.

"Will and I are so proud to have you and Emmie as official members of the family."

"Thanks, Helen. I can't express how much it means to me as well. This beautiful woman has made me the happiest man in the world today. I don't think it can get much better than this."

"Aww, it will get better. I think there are great things in store for your future. You just wait and see."

"Welcome to the family, man." Abby's husband Wyatt shook Cole's hand and gave him a hug.

"Between you and Ethan I'm finally starting to feel a little less outnumbered by all the women."

"Wyatt, I don't know who you're trying to kid. You've always been spoiled rotten by all the women in the family and you know it." Mom was insistent, and Wyatt didn't argue with her.

"Yes, ma'am, just as spoiled as I can be." He winked at Cole in passing.

Abby shook her head.

"Well, either way you look at it I think you make a perfect addition to the family, Cole. Just watching you two exchanging your vows today brought back such sweet memories of when me and Wyatt were married. Oh and watching daddy escort you down the aisle, Payton, brought tears to my eyes."

"Abby, me, too. It was all I could do to keep my composure."

Emmie emerged through the crowd of adults with Aidan and my niece Maggie.

"All the kids are challenging all the adults to a dance contest on the dance floor in five minutes. So be there or be square!"

Aidan came forward in his little suit and added his two cents.

"Yeah, be square!"

No one in my family turned down a challenge. Cole went around the tent grabbing as many neighbors and friends from the community of Pelican Beach to join us on the dance floor as possible. Even some of the old staff members from the Inn were there, along with Natalie, and some of our closest friends were all on the dance floor having a good time.

Later that evening when the last guest was gone, my siblings and our spouses remained under the tent with a glass of wine. We kicked our feet up and laughed and recalled the events of the day.

"We did it, babe. We pulled off the finest beach front wedding in all of Pelican Beach," Cole said.

"We sure did and now we can finally breathe a sigh of relief. No more planning, cake tasting, coordinating."

"That's right. Now, we can just walk into our happily ever after," he said.

"Cheers to our happily ever after."

We all clinked glasses to that one.

"Payton, I didn't realize the Pelican Beach News was going to be at the wedding. I'll bet tomorrow morning your pictures will be plastered all over the front cover of the paper. Matter of fact, let me look up your names now to see if anything pops up." Rebecca started searching through her phone.

"Cole, I know we invited Dale and his wife but did you ask them for a special column in the paper? I sure didn't."

"No, but Payton as small as this town is, Dale probably keeps his camera by his side at all times."

"That's a good point."

"Well, I can't find anything on my phone just yet, but we'll save you a few copies for when you get back from Tahiti."

"Thanks, Becks."

Ethan returned from checking on the kids up at the house to make sure they weren't driving their grandparents crazy.

"Okay, I've been biting my tongue all night, but who's going to fill me in on Cousin Jolene? I just saw her in the living room and 'oh boy' is all I can say!" Ethan said.

I caught Rebecca rolling her eyes from across the table and Abby laughing.

"Seriously. When we were kids, I remember anytime she ever came over your whole house was turned upside down for about a week. Then as soon as she would leave things would go back to normal again."

"See. Even Ethan remembers how crazy she was back then!" Abby said.

"Ethan, you need to repeat what you just said to our mother. It seems like everybody remembers the real Jolene except for her." I snuggled next to Cole. I was still on a wedding high and wasn't about to let anything of this spoil it for me. I had already made peace that if mom was happy with Jolene coming to help, then I would be happy.

"Payton, have you talked to her?" Abby asked.

"I've said all I'm going to say. If mom is happy then I say let her be. Besides, what's the worst that could happen?"

Abby and Rebecca looked at one another.

"Oh, come on. If it bothers you two that much, then maybe one of you should say something."

"The deed is done now. Jolene said her moving truck was arriving first thing in the morning." Abby threw back the last sip of her wine before finishing her thought.

"If you ask me I say she plans on making this her permanent residence."

"Abby, that's the wine talking. Mom said it was just to help out for a little while. Let's not get ahead of ourselves." That was the last thing our family needed.

"Well, if I may interject here. Whatever's going on with Cousin Jolene won't be resolved overnight but here's what I know for certain." Cole smiled at me.

"What do you know for certain, handsome?" I felt like a first time bride, so happy, and so in love.

"The beautiful Mrs. Payton Miller and I have plans of our own first thing in the morning. Those plans involve a first class flight to Tahiti, and I don't plan on missing one minute of it."

"Neither do I, babe...neither do I."

"Somebody hurry up and get them past the mushy stage, please," Wyatt called out.

"Oh, Wyatt, hush! There's nothing wrong with a little mush every now and again," Abby scolded her husband but they both loved the banter back and forth. I honestly think it was their way of flirting with each other.

She poured the last round of wine in everyone's glass.

"Come on, everybody. Raise your glasses one more time for the newlyweds. Payton and Cole, to a lifetime of love and happiness. We love you and wish you all the best! Cheers!"

All of our voices chimed, "Cheers!"

That night I finished packing my bags and thanked the heavens for another chance at love. I never put much stock in fairytales and happily ever afters. Not since I was a little girl at least. I figured as long as I was fairly healthy and happy then I had a lot to be thankful for. But, there's something I've adopted that's helped through the most difficult times. Never give up hope and always make room in your heart for second chances.

EPILOGUE: ALICE

"Cole, we have something important we want to share with you and Payton."

We sat across from one another in the living room. They both looked like they'd been kissed by the sun from their honeymoon in Tahiti. Cole looked a little fidgety and nervous.

"I thought this was a laid back get-together. You two seem rather serious."

I squeezed Stanley's hand.

"Do you want to share the news, sweetheart?"

"I think Cole should hear this from you."

Payton's eyes started to light up. You could tell she knew something was up.

"Well, son, we asked you and Payton to join us this evening so we could spend some time together."

Before I could finish Cole jumped in.

"Yeah, this was a good idea. We were planning on inviting you over once we got back but coming over to your place is even better. Hey, Stanley, maybe we'll get a chance to see your house since you and mom live in the same neighborhood."

He leaned over and commented to Payton, "Isn't that so funny how they live in the same neighborhood?"

She smiled while remaining focused on me and Stanley. "Oh, huh? Yes, sure, babe."

"Cole, there's more. While you were in Tahiti... Stanley and I got engaged."

His smile slowly began to fade.

"You did what?"

"We got engaged. Honey, I know it seems sudden but we're not getting any younger and well..."

Stanley locked eyes with me and finished my sentence.

"And we know this is what we want. We're in love and we're certain we want to spend the rest of our lives together."

"Aww, this is soooo sweet!" Payton began fanning her face to keep from tearing up.

Cole didn't seem as enthused.

"Can't say that I saw this coming. Whew, I don't even know what to say."

"Cole, you don't have to say anything. I'm the one who has some explaining to do. I should start by telling you about myself. It's the least I can do."

"With all due respect, I intended on getting to know you over time and through experience. Not during some brief exchange one evening right before you try to marry my mother."

"Cole! We didn't say we were eloping. Give him a chance and hear what Stanley has to say."

He leaned back and let out a deep breath.

"Alright, I'm listening."

"Well, for starters, I'm from a small little town in Mobile, Alabama."

"How did you end up in Florida?"

Cole rattled off a quick question as if he were conducting an interview.

"The military. I grew up in Alabama but my mother passed away when me and my brothers were young. I took on whatever responsibilities I could to help my father keep our family together. At the age of eighteen I followed dad's advice and joined the army. He encouraged us all to join. He said it would make men out of us and lead to a secure future."

"Hmm," Cole grunted.

"In the army I spent most of my time working with the Criminal Investigation Command. In that time frame I became pretty good at discerning between the liars and the scum bags versus the good guys. Do you know how I was able to decipher between the two?"

"No, sir, but I'm sure you're about to tell me." Cole sounded a little snarky.

"The liars had a way of nervously looking around when they were being dishonest. They never could look me in the eyes. It was always a tell tale sign."

Payton sat near the edge of the couch hanging on to every word Stanley spoke.

"You're not going to get any dishonesty out of me, Cole. I'm going to look you in the eyes and give it to you straight. I love your mother. I knew she was special from the moment I laid eyes on her. And, because I knew how special she was it made me nervous. I took my time and befriended her. As a matter of fact, I took so long to reveal my feelings for her, I almost lost her to another man. I'll bet she never told you about Mr. Lover Boy who tried to sweep her off her feet, did she?"

"No, sir."

I had to interject to make sure Cole understood my intentions.

"It wasn't a secret, Cole. I just know how you are when it comes to me having a love life. I didn't want to upset you."

"Okay, so you were friends for a while, someone else came along and posed a threat, and then you swooped in to win the grand prize. Got it. How this all came about really doesn't matter to me. No matter which way you slice it, you're still a stranger who's trying to marry my mother."

"Now, wait one minute. I've heard just about enough. I expected you to be surprised, Cole. I even expected you to have a lot of questions, as you should. That's what you do when you care about your family. But to be blatantly disrespectful is simply not like you. You're not listening to a word Stanley has to say."

"I am listening, but you have to admit this is kind of sudden."

"No, you're not listening! At least not with your heart. I get that you want what's best for me. But, you can't be the judge of how long we should wait before we get married. I didn't pass judgement when you and Payton decided to marry after knowing each other for a short time."

"She has a good point there," Payton murmured under her breath.

"Look, Cole, from one man to another, the one thing we have in common is the desire to see your mother happy. I have her best interest at heart whether you believe it or not. Perhaps our focus for now should be on getting to know each other better. We can always revisit this conversation later."

"Oh...no...we...can't! We will not put this conversation off until later. If you two are really focused on my happiness then hear me loud and clear. Stanley and I are getting married by the end of the year. We will merge households over the next few months and I will enjoy my Chamomile tea and pound cake, right here, with my husband every day if I want to."

Cole looked perplexed over the tea and cake but I'm sure Payton would fill him in later. I was putting my foot down. No one was getting in the way of my happiness. Not even my son.

"Okay," Cole responded.

"And, now that you got me all fired up let me tell you one more thing! Over these next five or six months, we will spend time together, we will continue to place an importance on family, as we always have, and Cole... you will get to know my best friend Stanley and hopefully grow to love him just as much as I do!"

I stopped and took a moment. It had been a long time since I felt so passionate and worked up about something of this magnitude.

In the most calm voice I could muster up I exhaled and said, "Gentlemen, have I made myself clear?"

They answered in unison, "Yes, ma'am."

Cole slowly revealed his pearly white teeth and shook his head.

"What are you smiling about?" I asked.

"I haven't seen that fire in you since daddy was alive. You used to get so spit fire mad at him sometimes... you were a force to be reckoned with. He used to always say that's how he knew you loved him so much."

All the tension was released as soon as I heard Cole mention his dad.

"He sure did, son."

"You've been holding all that passion inside for all these years. It's almost like that part of you died when daddy passed away."

"I never thought about it that way before."

"Well, it's obvious to me. If Stanley makes you feel this alive again, then who am I to stand in the way?"

The flood gates let loose. I felt so relieved. It had been a long time since I felt like I could wring Cole's neck one minute, then turn around and hug him right after.

"Aww, come here. Give me a hug. I knew you would understand."

"Oh, thank God." Payton was just as relieved as I was.

The icing on the cake for me was watching Cole extend his hand to Stanley.

"I meant what I said earlier, Cole. Your mother's happiness is what's most important to me."

"I'm going to hold you to it, sir."

Stanley chuckled. "I bet you will."

If my late husband was watching over us that day I know he would've been proud of Cole and happy for me. It takes a lot of courage to make room in your heart to love again. But, when it's right, it's right, and nothing should stand in the way.

Ready to continue on to Book four, Christmas at Pelican Beach? Click here or turn the page to learn more!

NEW TROPICAL BREEZE SERIES!

When Meg Carter advances a year's worth of rent on a beach house, she's shocked to land and discover it's been sold at an auction.

The new owner, Parker Wilson, is forty, a real estate investor, and ready to get the property flip underway.

When Meg digs her heels in and refuses to leave, will this drive them to become fierce enemies?

Or will they find common ground and potentially become sweet lovers?

Pull up your favorite beach chair and watch as Meg and Parker's story unfolds in this new Bahama Breeze Series today!

Tropical Breeze Series:

Tropical Encounter: Book 1
Tropical Escape: Book 2
Tropical Moonlight: Book 3
Tropical Summers: Book 4
Tropical Brides: Book 5

THE SOLOMONS ISLAND SERIES

Come visit us on Solomons Island. A beach series with stories of heartwarming love, friendships, and even a little drama in this small-town saga.

With multiple love stories to follow, and a community that sticks together, the cast of characters on Solomons are sure to keep you coming back for more!

Book one begins with Clara and Mike's love story. So,

pull up a beach chair, your favorite beverage, and fall in love with Solomons Island.

Solomons Island Series:

Beachfront Inheritance: Book 1

Beachfront Promises: Book 2

Beachfront Embrace: Book 3

Beachfront Christmas: Book 4

Beachfront Memories: Book 5

Beachfront Secrets: Book 6

THE PELICAN BEACH SERIES

Pack your bags and enjoy beautiful sunsets at Pelican Beach! Like anywhere you may visit, there will be a little drama, and maybe even some unwanted competition. But the main dish being served in this series is love sweet love!

Pelican Beach Series:

The Inn at Pelican Beach: Book 1

Created with Vellum

Made in the USA
Middletown, DE
17 November 2023